Helen Jones is a 90-year-old retired widow who has lived abroad for several years.

Mrs. Jones handmakes dolls for severely disabled children abroad and has a dog, Socks. She has written many children's fables. These stories have lain in a folder for years. Finally, Mrs. Jones, with encouragement from several friends and acquaintances, decided to submit two of her stories for consideration. She lives in Woodbridge and has two daughters and five grandchildren.

I want to thank Barbara Anniballi and Linda Satlin, who believed in my stories and encouraged me to attempt to publish them.

Helen Jones

LICORICE AND BLACK JACK

AUSTIN MACAULEY PUBLISHERS™

LONDON • CAMBRIDGE • NEW YORK • SHARJAH

Ordering Information
Quantity sales: Special discounts are available on quantity purchases by corporations, associations, and others. For details, contact the publisher at the address below.

Publisher's Cataloging-in-Publication data
Jones, Helen
Licorice and Black Jack

ISBN 9798889101697 (Paperback)
ISBN 9798889101703 (Hardback)
ISBN 9798889101710 (ePub e-book)
ISBN 9798889103936 (Audiobook)

Library of Congress Control Number: 2023918407

www.austinmacauley.com/us

First Published 2024
Austin Macauley Publishers LLC
40 Wall Street, 33rd Floor, Suite 3302
New York, NY 10005
USA

mail-usa@austinmacauley.com
+1 (646) 5125767

I want to thank Rebecca Morgan and Brian Basset, who made technology appear effortless, and without whom my book would have never been possible.

Licorice and Black Jack were Bombay Cats who were brothers. They were born aboard a massive sailing ship while at sea with their other three littermates. Both cats had shiny black coats, and sparkling yellow eyes which shone with mischievous intent. They were identical, except for their tails. Licorice had a straight tail, while Black Jack's tail was crooked, having been crushed when he caught it on a grappling hook while trying to chase a fat rat. The rat got away, but Black Jack became scarred forever.

When they looked exactly alike, the cats got away with many shenanigans, because neither one would accept the blame, but a crooked tail made it easy to spot the difference between them and the fun times of faking identities were over. This made Black Jack hate rats more than ever! From that moment on, Black Jack swore vengeance on all rats, wherever they might be!

Unlike other cats that are usually territorial, Licorice and Black Jack were always together. When the seas became choppy and rough and high waves tossed the ship from side to side, it often felt as though they were going to drown from the massive waves that poured over the vessel's deck. Everyone and everything was soaking wet, and the cats huddled together with their littermates.

Stormy weather made them feel incredibly close to one another in a way unknown to landlubber cats. From birth, the duo became inseparable. They adored each other and even shared every tidbit they found. Never once did either one take the other's meal.

When the waters were becalmed and the ship stalled and drifted from lack of sailing winds, life was usually dull. After the crew scrubbed the vessel clean, repaired the sails, and mended the ropes, there was little left to do but wait for good headwinds. Seeing their shipmates' boredom, the cats devised ways to entertain them.

Their tricks were a fun and funny way of making the sailors want to give them tasty choice bits from their plates when they ate. They befriended the ship's "Cookie" and spent much time hanging out in the galley. They danced on the galley counter and drove the cook mad trying to shoo them off, but they usually wound up getting first dibs on everything he prepared. They rushed to the mess room during meals to scarf up any morsel dropped or passed to them under the table by the sailors.

They were rarely reprimanded, even when they peered down the hatch and got underfoot when the crew was trying to load or offload cargo.

Sailing was not always fun, as everyone claimed. There was much work to do, like scrubbing the deck daily to clean off the barnacles, seaweed, marine growth, and shipworms. Life at sea was tough as well as dull, and the sailors needed entertainment occasionally.

When Licorice and Black Jack were not licking their shiny coats, they performed wacky antics to make the sailors laugh until tears ran down their faces and their stomachs ached from laughing. The cats would climb up on the ropes, chasing one another, and slide down while making little mewing sounds. They tumbled, scooted, ran, and chased each other until they were exhausted.

They scampered up the ship's yardarm and pounced on the head of any unsuspecting sailor as he passed. The seamen took to wearing thick wool caps to protect themselves from being scratched by the cat's claws when one suddenly landed. Licorice and Black Jack curled up into little balls and rolled around the ship's deck. They thumped on the sailor's legs as if they were bowling balls. Sometimes they had yowling contests to determine which one of the brothers could screech the loudest or the highest. The sailors would wager pints of ale on which one would win.

As a special treat for a favorite sailor, the cats would choose a different hamper nightly in which to sleep. That made for many a bet to determine which of the crewmen would be selected. The cats were warm and fuzzy, and their little bodies provided warmth. They purred and buzzed softly, sending the lucky old salt gently to sleep.

The two cats were the favorites of the seafarers. The other members of the litter were quiet and subdued. They stayed to themselves, hunted for their prey, and acted as one would expect any self-respecting feline to behave. Not so Licorice and Black Jack! They provided great entertainment for the bored crew, but they also proved to be accomplished ratters.

They furtively roamed the ship and raided every crack and crevice in which rodents might hide. After their forages, the boat stayed rat and mice free for the rest of that voyage. No matter what port the vessel visited, and regardless of how many rats or mice sneaked aboard, none were in evidence when the ship pulled into the harbor. Everyone loved Licorice and Black Jack.

The Captain was so proud of his ownership of the cats that he had his ship's figurehead carved to resemble Licorice and Black Jack. He also commissioned a world-famous flag maker to sew a flag for the main mast with Licorice and Black Jack's likeness. Among seamen, the cat's reputation traveled far and wide. Every sea dog on the seven seas knew that Licorice and Black Jack were the best ones in the world to rid a vessel of unwanted vermin.

Each time the ship would enter a harbor, some ship captain would approach the boat and offer to buy one or the other cat. They proffered bulging sacks of coin for them. The Captain always refused. He said he would be willing to sell one of Licorice and Black Jacks' littermates, but he made it clear that the two were not for sale for any amount of money.

Once a sailor from another ship was caught red-handed trying to steal one of the brothers, but the crew rapidly ran him off. The cats were valuable team members and were guarded closely when the ship docked at any new port, for fear that some unscrupulous brigand would steal them.

The ship members never dreamed that one of their team would stoop so low as to take their prized merrymakers and all-time great ratters!

However, there was an unsavory member of the crew who was named Klutz Hare Brain. He was always doing something underhanded. He cheated at cards regularly and needed watching whenever he tossed dice or played any game. Most crew members refused to play with him as he wasn't honest about anything.

He was lazy and never pulled his weight. Whenever the ship was fighting high seas, he claimed to have trouble with his stomach and could never man the crow's nest or climb the forecastle. Klutz was always the last to appear during an emergency. He never helped lift the bales of cargo in any port unless he was forced to, and not once did he offer to lend a hand with any of the ship chores unless a senior officer demanded it.

Previously, Klutz had been flogged by the First Boson's mate with a cat o' nine tails for attempting to steal a valuable item from the Captain's cabin. The only reason the crew didn't throw him overboard was that the ship was short of hands. One day, shortly after that incident, a crewman caught Klutz stealing personal items from several crew members and stuffing the valuables in his rucksack.

At that point, the ship's Captain took a vote among the crew members. They gave him several choices: either he could be strapped to the yardarm, flogged, keelhauled, made to walk the plank, or leave the ship with only the clothes on his back. The crew's vote was for him to either walk the plank or clear out. There was going to be no negotiating about that.

Klutz was glad that the yardarm, keelhauling, and flogging options were not approved. He couldn't stand the pain, didn't want to drown, and hated to work, so making up his mind quickly, he decided he would take off at the next port. All of the options given by the Captain were dreadful, and he especially didn't want punishment by keelhauling or plank walking. There were sharks in the surrounding water, to say nothing of the fact that he couldn't swim.

He was aware of how valuable and loved the cats were. He wanted to get revenge on the Captain and crew for making him leave, and he knew that taking them would be the worst thing he could do by far. Further, he needed to obtain as much money from their sale as he could because he hadn't completed his voyage contract and the Captain refused to give him any wages. He was only half-way through the trip when they caught him stealing.

While everyone was sleeping, he crept around the snoozing men and found a strong fishing net in the dark. Fortunately for him, that night neither cat was curled up with a shipmate; the brothers were nestled on the ship's deck. He trapped Licorice and Black Jack within the net. He also tried snagging the other three cats, but they hid in the hold of the ship, and he had to leave before the crew members caught him.

When Licorice and Black Jack disappeared, the sailors searched every inch of the ship. Then they looked in every inn, doorway, and alleyway in town. They were devastated and posted a reward for the cats.

As luck would have it, an older woman was closing her shutters when Klutz passed by her house with the squirming bag, so when the sailors walked past her home, she told them what happened. From her description, they realized it was Klutz and placed a hefty bounty on his head.

They shared the bounty papers with every ship in the harbor and asked all the sailors to tell everyone what had occurred. Once a thief, always a thief, they thought. If he was guilty of such a dreadful deed, he would most likely do something evil again, and they hoped he would be recognized. They wanted him caught in the worst way.

Once he had the cats snared in his net, Klutz transferred them to a gunny sack because he knew they would hurt themselves while entangled in the nets, trying to get out. He trudged off through the suburbs into Woebegone Swamp. He walked a long distance and finally went to sleep on a moss bed after tying the bag with the cats to a tree. Licorice and Black Jack were so tired from their struggle that they gave up and nodded off, too.

When Klutz awoke, he had to work hard to retrieve the bag that was jumping again, furiously tussled by the cats that wanted to be released. The thief was hungry and thirsty, and knowing he had no money to buy food, he decided to sell the cats to the first buyer that came along who would give him a decent offer.

After a while, he met an old crone. She was Hexine, the witch. She stopped him and asked him what he had wiggling in the bag. He told her, and carefully opened it to let her peek inside. She was ecstatic because Hexine's place was overrun with mice and she was hoping that an experienced cat could take care of her problem.

She requested him to sell her just one of the cats, but he refused. They had already given him too much trouble, trying to scratch and bite their way out of the sack, and he wanted to be rid of them pronto. It was either purchase both or "No deal," so she agreed to buy the pair of them. They haggled over the price for an extended period, until finally, Hexine gave Klutz a fat bag of silver.

After telling the witch what the cat's names were, he went off merrily with pockets jingling, thinking of the delicious meal he was going to have. He was delighted by the price he got for the "little devils" and was glad to be rid of them. Also, he was happy that he had punished his shipmates and the Captain for mistreating him. "They'll never have a rat-free ship again," he thought, as Hexine shuffled off with the bag containing the cats under her arm.

Hexine the Witch lived in a hut deep in Woebegone Forest. The cats longed for their old home. Once they were with the witch, the cats wrought havoc daily, and at times they drove her to the brink of madness! They used their nails for ripping her curtains to shreds. They scratched the chair legs and tables, chewed the already threadbare carpet, and destroyed the cushions on the chairs and sofa. They even clawed the covers of her ancient magic books to shreds. They chased every bird and butterfly out of her yard and made life miserable for all the rabbits, woodchucks, raccoons, squirrels, chipmunks, and even the deer that once played and rambled freely. They were the bane of everyone's existence.

After chasing all the woodland creatures away, the place became too quiet for their liking. They missed being at sea and all the jolly, roaring, rollicking good times they once had with the raucous, fun-loving sailors. They also craved being fed tidbits when the sailors ate and missed nibbling up the crumbs that fell from the dining mess table.

There was nothing like that happening while living with Hexine. The crone seldom fed them, due to her forgetfulness. At first, the cats, renowned as prize mousers on the ship and throughout the land, chased the mice. A short time after their arrival, they rid Hexine's place of all the mice that overran her hut. Lickety-split, just like that, they were all gone. But after the shack was mouse-free, Licorice and Black Jack had nothing to eat.

Hexine rented the cats to the villagers who had mice problems. Renting them worked for a while because they were excellent hunters, but the cat's antics were too much for the folks. Every renter returned the devilish duo post-haste with a bill or two for destroyed furniture. Hexine couldn't afford to pay for the many damages that the cats wrought. She just wanted them to go away.

Licorice and Black Jack thought that a fantastic idea too, so one day, after missing a week's grub, they decided to take off to look for some other place to live. Off they scat, with never a thought further than finding a substantial meal again.

Hexine didn't miss those rabble-rousing rascals; her only regret was the money they used to make for her. She also began to spot several mice running about her hut. *Oh, dear*, she thought, *Not that problem again! Lordy, Lordy, what an ungodly mess. You have cats, they destroy everything; then you have mice, and they stink up the place and chew up everything. Is there no end to it?*

Licorice and Black Jack strolled down a road which was a reasonable distance from Hexine's place. They came upon a busy roadside inn. The kitchen smells were tantalizing. They drooled with hunger. The cats crept up silently and entered the dining room. They sneaked under the table of a jolly-looking, fat traveler.

On his red and white checkered tablecloth sat hot rolls, butter, a pot of jam, potatoes, carrots, brussels sprouts, candied yams, a large boat of gravy, cherry pie, a big tankard of ale, and an enormous baked leg of mutton to boot! The meat sizzled, singing, "Take me, take me," to the brothers. It emitted the best aroma the cats had smelled since leaving the ship. "Hallelujah! We've hit the jackpot!"

After the happy traveler adjusted his napkin on his neck and was about to cut into the meat, the cats jumped up and pulled down on the edge of the tablecloth. Down fell the food all over the floor! It was everywhere! Licorice and Black Jack hastily grabbed the mutton leg between them and dashed out of the inn door before the innkeeper or the patron who had bought the food could stop them.

Off they sped into the woods. The fat man was too obese to catch the fleeing brothers, and the innkeeper couldn't leave his business for fear of being robbed by the other travelers. The fat man was no longer jolly; he was screaming to high heaven at the innkeeper. He demanded his money back. He accused the innkeeper of letting his cats run riot and not keeping an eye on the greedy, nasty little creatures. He told the owner he should feed his cats so they wouldn't be so gluttonous as to steal an honest person's meal right off the table!

The innkeeper denied ownership of the cats and refused to give the traveler his money back. He told him he should have been more careful and paid attention to what was going on around him. A huge fight ensued. The fat man pummeled the innkeeper with his fists and his empty tankard, and the innkeeper smashed the traveler on the head with a frying pan he held in his hand. Both had black eyes from popping and slugging each other with their fists.

Finally, they slipped on the spilled gravy and fell heavily to the ground, spreading the food mess further around and ruining their clothes beyond repair. Without paying for their meals in the tavern, the other visitors grabbed some food and ran out quickly. They stepped over both men, who were continuing to fight, and departed with the two fighters rolling around in the thick brown gravy and the leftovers of the smashed, slippery mess.

Licorice and Black Jack found a beautiful quiet spot under a massive oak tree. There, they stopped and ate until there was only a clean bone to show for their endeavors. They were full and happy for the first time since being taken from the ship. "Now," they thought, "this is the way to go." They planned to steal all their meals in the future, and in the same manner. No more scrounging for crumbs or hunting for "Maybe we'll find an occasional mouse to eat." They determined that only the very best was good enough for them.

With their bellies full of the tasty mutton, the brothers fell asleep. When they awoke, it was daybreak. They wondered where they were going to get their next meal. After life with Hexine, they did not want any more of the batty old crone's miss-meal craziness.

They were glad she had not put a spell on either of them because they had heard her talking to a passerby as she asked if he had seen her "walking stick." The stranger shook his head and rapidly sped off in a frightened way. If she had found the rod, she might have been able to jinx people and animals. "We're glad we are no longer there," they thought.

Looking around at their surroundings, they discovered a large cart with two dray horses drinking water at the edge of a small pool. The wagon had a burlap cover over the top, which the cats thought would serve as concealment and transportation to the nearest town. They didn't want the innkeeper to find them. Heaven only knows what he would do to them if he did!

Of course, riding sure beat walking. They also reasoned they could probably stay in the wagon as a safe hiding place until they could figure out what their next move would be. Quickly, the cats scampered into it.

After hiding under several bags of what felt like fur, the wagon started to roll. Looking at the old horses that were driving the cart, they expected a slow, leisurely tour.

Not so! The driver was beating the nags and making them move way too fast for them to jump off and escape, so they just had to hang on for dear life. They were bumped, jostled, jounced, bounced, and wobbled from side to side.

In no time, both cats got bruised. Their hair became caught on huge fragments on the truck's bed and was ripped out in clumps. Even when sailing, in no manner were they ever brutalized in this way. No storm ever made them this sick. They just wanted to get out, but that was impossible.

Little did they know that the driver was Grifter O. Reilly, a man who owned the largest butcher shop and fish market in the country. People came from miles around to purchase his fresh produce. He always had the most excellent food available in the entire country. Everything he sold was crisp and beautiful.

He would entice cats into his shop by offering them newly killed fish heads and innards, and dogs with lovely, juicy beef bones. All his fellow shopkeepers thought of him as a kind, generous type of fellow, for he always had many animals around his shop. He especially seemed to care genuinely for stray animals.

The truth was, Grifter made extra money catching and capturing cats and dogs for their beautiful pelts. Not only did he want the hides, but he wanted animals for their meat. Grifter would pass it off to buyers as exotic viands imported from distant countries. He called the cat meat Roof Rabbit and the dog meat Blockade Filet of Mutton.

Mostly everyone rushed to his shop when they were entertaining important people or dignitaries. The imported food always made an impression on the visitors. Every homemaker wanted to outdo the other when it came to providing a lavish spread, and their solution was to buy provisions from Grifter.

The vendor became most excited when he could locate a large dog or a litter of cats with the same markings and coat type. Those kinds of critters would provide larger pelts and would earn him a lot of money. The more lustrous an animal's fur was, the more it could be made into an attractive fur item for the wealthy men and women of the town, and the more he could get for it.

The butcher/fishmonger would sell skins to a crooked old clothing designer named Yenta, who lived at the end of Furrier's Lane. His fellow garment makers disliked the tailor because he could always find the rare fur they could not. He refused to divulge his source or share his secret. Although they searched everywhere, they were unable to discover anything like the fur he used.

Once he made an article, it was one of a kind. They could never compete with him. The pelts made beautiful hats, collars, fur muffs, and sometimes fur coats, when he could buy matching skins or ones that were large enough. Yenta charged a fortune for his wares. He passed the dog's fur off as Mongolian Wolf and the cat's as Raccoon Dog. Every woman in town wanted something fabricated by Yenta. Of course, none of them was aware that this fur came from domesticated pets!

Many of the cats and dogs were disappearing from the homes of the townspeople. No one could figure out what happened to them, and they only knew there were far fewer pets than there had ever been. They never asked themselves why. They just knew the animals had up and gone.

A town without cats and dogs wasn't so pleasant. There were no cats to chase mice and no dogs to bark and warn you of harm. Those animals had a definite place in the world. The citizens wondered what they could do to attract or raise more of the kind of creatures that would stay around and not vanish into thin air!

Finally, the cart came to a jolting halt. Both cats were thrown into the wagon's front frame and hit so severely that they were knocked out! Grifter pulled back the burlap cover to retrieve the bags of fur and discovered the unconscious cats. "Gadzooks," he chuckled, "look what I found! A pair of matching cats! They'll bring a pretty sum. Yenta has to pay me some serious coin for them."

He picked them up by the scruff of their necks and rushed them into the back of his shop. The vendor looked them over and discovered that they had clumps of their hair missing. "What a mess," he said. "I could use them for meat, toss them out, or now that I think about it, I could put them in a cage, feed them, and wait until their coats grow out and become shiny again. Then I'll skin them and sell them to my friend, Yenta."

Grifter shoved the still unconscious cats into a large cage in a locked room. Then he drove to Yenta's with the bags of fur, haggled about every pelt, and got his money.

When he described the two black cats he had, Yenta was delighted. Having received an order for a collar and muff from a well-to-do woman, he had not been able to fill the request up till now. The furrier asked Grifter when he could expect the skins and was told that it would take some time and to be patient, as they were well worth the wait.

Licorice and Black Jack finally woke up. They wondered how they got into this current fix. The cage had a large lock on the door, and the bars were so close they could not hope to squeeze through. They were in an all-time mess, that was for sure!

Grifter returned to his store, stabled his old horses, and opened to customers. He worked all day. Business was brisk. Lots of customers came and bought a heap of fish and meat. Grifter thought, "Life is good."

He finally looked in on the cats. There they were, but they were not a pretty sight. He thought, "Wait until I fatten them up. Their coats will shine, and I will make a mint." He filled a plate full of first-class fish and slid it through the slot at the front of the cage door. He decided he would not open it for fear of their escaping. He also had a removable tray which he could take out to clean their waste.

Licorice and Black Jack's golden eyes glared at Grifter with hatred. If looks could kill, he would have been a goner. The cats ate the fish, which was delicious, with little appetite, but they knew they needed strength to escape.

Grifter left them for the night, after covering the cage with a sheet and locking the room door so no one could hear the cats' pitiful cries for help. Licorice and Black Jack were heartbroken. They tried getting out of the cage, but to no avail. Finally, they settled down for the night, curled up, and had a fitful sleep.

The following day Grifter arrived again, whistling a happy tune. He was holding a mackerel tabby cat by the scruff of its neck. The cat was kicking, crying, and mewing for "all get out," but Grifter ignored its wails. He took the cat into another room and slammed the door.

Immediately, Licorice and Black Jack heard a thump, then silence. What on earth happened, wondered the brothers.

The fishmonger came out in an hour or so with a black and white pelt thrown over his shoulder. He also had a massive plate of meat! "Great googly-woogilies," thought the cats. "He killed that tabby! What on earth is going on? Is that what is in our future?"

They frantically tried scratching their way out of the cage. They broke several of their claws, but their attempts were futile. "What a horrible set of events this has turned out to be," they thought.

For many days it was the same story. Although fed, they had lost their appetites and ate only to stay alive. The fish/meat vendor would come in for three things: first, was to feed and water them; second, was to empty their waste tray; and third, worst of all, was to bring some unfortunate animal into the back room to slaughter it.

Grifter would put his hands through the cage bars in order to feel the cats' weight and fur. They snapped, hissed, and bit him, and pushed themselves to the furthest corner of the cage so he couldn't touch them. It was a nightmare for the brothers. They were nervous wrecks but couldn't devise a means of escape.

One morning, an old lady, the Widow Mims, was passing by when she spotted Grifter holding a large brown dog by the scruff of his neck. She recognized it as being the property of her neighbor because the widow had dog sat with the animal several times when the near-by resident needed to be out of town. She wondered if the dog had done something naughty and Grifter was punishing him. By the time she hobbled up to question what he was doing, he had already entered his shop door, closed it, and disappeared into his back room.

Widow Mims went to her neighbor, Citizen Simon Clemmons, and asked him if his dog, Toby, was around. The only reason she asked, she said, was because she thought that she saw Grifter carrying him into his store.

Citizen Clemmons whistled for his hound. "That's odd," he said. "He always comes when I whistle. Now, what mischief has that hound done?" He thought the dog might have annoyed Grifter, or maybe, like the compassionate fellow that he was, Grifter might have been giving him a treat.

He thanked Widow Mims and went to see the fish/meat vendor to retrieve his dog.

When Simon arrived at the store, Grifter was standing behind his fish/meat counter with a clean, fresh apron. He asked Clemmons what he wanted to buy. The man said, "Nothing today," and asked if he had seen his dog, Toby. The vendor denied seeing him, so Simon asked him to please direct the animal home if he spotted him. He said he and his son planned to go hunting the next day, and they would need the dog. Grifter smiled and said he would be glad to look out for him.

The following day, Toby was still missing. Simon went to see Widow Mims and questioned her again about the dog. The widow stated that she wasn't mistaken, and she knew for sure she had seen Grifter with him.

By this time, Simon was becoming suspicious of the fish/meat vendor's response. He had known Widow Mims for a long time and found her to be one of the most honest people in the town. Simon felt she would have no ax to grind, telling him some tall tale about his dog. He decided to get to the bottom of the puzzle.

Not able to go hunting, Simon walked up and down the crooked streets and alleyways of the town, whistling for Toby, but Toby was not in evidence. He even went to the docks and queried all the sailors who were in port. It took the entire day of searching, with no luck.

Never, in all the time he had owned the dog, did he fail to come when summoned. Toby was five years old, not a puppy, and not up to any silly, young dog tricks. He was a sensible dog who was his faithful buddy and the county's best hunting dog. "Now, what on earth has happened to him?" he wondered.

Simon waited until nightfall, then crept around to Grifter's shop. The business was closed for the evening. All was quiet, with only the dim light from the street lamps, lit by the lamplighter earlier. There was so much fog that no one could see his hand before his face.

He was sure Grifter wouldn't be able to see him creeping about on his property. Simon went around to the back of the building and peered through the dirty window.

To his dismay and disgust, he saw some hides on a table, and one, he was sure, had been Toby's! "Good Lord, this is what has happened to all the missing dogs and cats in the town! What to do?"

Simon rushed to the police station. A policeman was at the desk, reclining in a chair, feet up, reared back, reading a paper. When Toby's owner told the story of the missing dog, he was not impressed. He said, "Simon, dogs go missing all the time in this town. Some visiting sailor has probably stolen them!"

That was too much for Citizen Clemmons. He asked the policeman if he could speak to the Chief of Police. The officer turned red, huffed, and puffed, and tried to discourage Simon from seeing his supervisor. "Now!" Simon shouted. The policeman rose slowly from his seat and told another officer to get the chief.

When the big "Poohbah" arrived, Simon related his story again. Chief Goodfellow was easy to convince because he had both a cat and a dog that went missing some time ago, and he was never able to discover what happened to them. His wife mourned for them and had never stopped lamenting the loss of her pets.

Simon and the chief hightailed over to Grifter's shop, and the chief, too, looked through the window. As before, on a table were several pelts belonging to cats and dogs that had been reported missing.

The chief went to the town judge and got a warrant straightaway. That in hand, he and a squad of officers broke down the shop door and entered.

Previously, Licorice and Black Jack saw Grifter holding a large book where he wrote notes about every stolen cat and dog, skinned and sold. He kept the ledger on a shelf above the cage which contained the two cats.

The cats saved some of the mutton fat from their meals and hid it in the rear of their enclosure. They then physically sat in front of it whenever the merchant was around. When Grifter was out of the room they would rub the grease up and down on the railing. Eventually, the bars of the cage became slippery with the oil. Licorice was able to reach one paw through it and raise it. Once done, both cats slipped out quietly.

Knowing the room's main door was locked, there was little hope of escaping through it unless Grifter left it open when he entered. He never did. They stood on each other's shoulders and pulled the book down. They pushed it into a large crevice below a cabinet. They returned to the cage and reversed their actions by slipping the bar down on the holding cell.

When Sheriff Goodfellow and Simon raided the shop, the cats started mewing and caterwauling without end. The chief wondered what the racket was. He soon found out!

Once freed, the cats jumped out of the cage and slid the book out from its hiding place; they pushed it toward Simon and the chief. The evidence was plain and simple enough to put him and Klutz in jail and throw away the key.

"The information within was all that the judge needed to convict those rascals," said the sheriff. The cats were the heroes of the day!

Through the shop, the officers went into the back rooms. They searched and discovered several skins on a large table in the rear of the store. Simon was heartbroken to find Toby's hide in that place.

The chief was enraged, but he decided to take Licorice and Black Jack home to live with him and his wife, Lolly. He thought if he could not find the rightful owners, then the cats would be a comfort to his family for the rest of their days.

He confiscated the ledger and all the pelts for evidence. Next, they went to Grifter's house and banged loudly on the door. He was livid about being awakened at such an ungodly hour! "An honest man needs his sleep," he said.

"Yes," said the chief, "an honest one does, but you are anything but that, and I am here to arrest you for slaughtering dogs and cats!"

Grifter was stunned by the discovery. Being the unsavory fellow he was, he immediately involved Yenta in the scheme. He proceeded to spill the beans about all the adverse events and their skullduggery. The chief dispatched several officers to arrest Yenta, put him in the police wagon, and bring him to the police station.

Both Grifter and Yenta were placed in separate cells in the jailhouse to await trials. Each claimed the other was guilty and denied any culpability in the crimes.

Meanwhile, Klutz, the thief, had settled in the town, and had a job as a stable hand sweeping out horse waste. In his travels, he had gambled away or squandered all of his ill-gotten gains from the sale of Licorice and Black Jack. The thief had no money left and no way of making any, as he lacked any skills. He could not ask for another job on a vessel because the Captain had kept his ship's papers so could not produce any.

Further, although the seaman was afraid word had spread of his past antics, he was unaware that the sheriff had hung a Wanted poster of Klutz in the town's police station. Anyone coming and going could see it and would yearn for the sum of 1,000 gold doubloons!

That was a massive fortune! How unfortunate it would be if someone saw him because he would then be reported to the authorities! The reward money would give that person security forever if he used the money wisely and spent it frugally.

After the chief arrived home, he woke his wife, Lolly. She was not in a great frame of mind because it was still very early, but she was a policeman's wife and knew their life was not always on the clock. She came into the kitchen to find out what he needed.

He then relayed all the happenings and showed her the cage with the black cats. She squealed with delight! She had sorely missed her pets, and this was a fantastic gift from her husband.

The chief told her he was not sure to whom they belonged, so if a person came forward and could prove ownership, she would have to give them up. She agreed and hoped the day would never arrive when she would have to lose them.

Mrs. Goodfellow kept them caged for several days to determine their dispositions. Licorice and Black Jack behaved wonderfully. They were genuinely grateful for being saved from that wicked killer and decided they would not spring any antics on this kind woman.

She finally thought she could trust them around the house, so she let them roam all over. They did not pounce on anything, steal any food, or scratch her furniture. They were unbelievably self-controlled. She fed them juicy morsels and tidbits and cuddled them every free moment she could, and they tolerated the excess of affection, but only for her sake. They were independent cats, after all!

She bought gold leashes and two jeweled collars and strutted with them all about the town. The cats were unaccustomed to being leashed, but they thought it was better than being caged or adorning some rich lady's collar or hat!

One day, while strolling past the docks, Klutz spied them with Lolly. He did not know she was the police chief's wife, so he thought he would snatch them again and make some more money. "What good fortune," he thought.

He dashed up to Lolly and yanked their leashes out of her hand. The cats, recognizing Klutz, jumped on him, screeching to high heaven, and scratched him badly. During the uproar, people in the street noticed the fray and recognized the chief's wife.

They came immediately to her rescue. They grappled Klutz to the ground as the cats tore at him, and sat on him while a youngster ran for the police. The law enforcement arrived quickly and took Klutz into custody.

A sailor from the ship on which Licorice and Black Jack had lived was also passing by at that time. He recognized the cats and told Lolly the story of their theft by Klutz. Lolly was disheartened because she had fallen in love with the brothers, but she knew she could not keep them if they belonged to someone else. She gave the seaman her address and asked him to notify his ship's Captain. He said he would.

She went to the jailhouse, and lo and behold, there was a wanted poster with Klutz's name on it. "Land o' Goshen, what terrible luck," she thought. "Now I really do have to give them up!"

The ship's Captain rushed to Lolly's house and retrieved his stolen cats. He was as happy to see the brothers as they were to see him. He knew that Mrs. Goodfellow would miss having Licorice and Black Jack around, so he offered to give her two of their littermates.

She was content with the offer, even though she had become extremely fond of the two. She did not know that their sisters were really much better behaved and mannered than they were.

Because Widow Mims told Simon Clemmons about Toby, and Simon notified the police of the horrible events, the town awarded them each 1,000 doubloons equally.

The wealthy townspeople, being mortified that they were wearing the town's cats and dogs on their persons, decided to stop wearing fur in the future. After discovering they had unknowingly ingested dog and cat meat, other citizens became vegetarians, remembering that they had even served the meat to their distinguished friends. UGH!

Licorice and Black Jack practically ran to the ship. Happy happy day! They could not express all their delight at being aboard a sailing vessel again. Once more, they would be with their seamen buddies. A sailor's life was definitely for them! Being a landlubber was very dangerous for the health of a cat.

Licorice and Black Jack in Trouble Again

Once again, Licorice and Black Jack are aboard their ship and at sea. Those rascally felines, after so many frightening, harrowing adventures, are happy to be back. They feel comfortable in their surroundings. No matter how rough the sea, the ship, the Fair Winds was their home and the only place they could feel they belonged. They were sure all the landlubber cats were happy living ashore, but not them, no. Only aboard the sailing ship could they find happiness and contentment.

When the cats were discovered and saved by Chief Goodfellow and brought to his house to live with his wife, Lolly, they were beyond grateful. To be back on the ship was even better. They thought we are not used to being cozened by a lady parading us up and down the town on gold leashes for everyone to ooh and aah! They thought we are cats, not dogs or baby dolls. They just wanted to roam the full range of the beautiful ship.

The sound of the wind slapping the canvas sails, keening ha, ha, ha of the circulating seagulls, the whistle and squeak of a school of passing dolphins was beyond description. The grunts, snorts, and barks of whales, the squeaking of the ropes as they restrained the sails from steering the ship where it was to go. Seeing the flying fish with iridescent wings that sparkled and shone in the sunlight was a sight to behold—smelling the salt air and having sea breezes ruffle your fur. There is nothing that could rival it. That's the life pure and simple that would please any seafaring cat!

Licorice and Black Jack were up to their old tricks. The sailors could hardly contain themselves having the prankish duo back in their midst. There had never been a sadder time for the crew than when Klutz stole them.

The rats and mice had run rampant during the feline's absence. Their two sisters were given in trade to Lolly Goodfellow for them. The sale left only one elderly mother cat and one sister to patrol the ship. Neither cat was the hunter that Licorice and Black Jack were. The rodents become so encouraged with the lack of being appropriately hunted that they frolicked up and down the deck, scaled the rigging, masts, and cables, left their unpleasant droppings and odor in the Captain's cabin, and ran gleefully all over. They made their home in the food goods in the hold of the ship. They ripped open the bags of rice and grain being transported and ate to their heart's content. There was not a place they didn't invade.

When the cats returned, they put an end to the foolishness of the pests. The life of every mouse and rat came to a swift conclusion, except one unusually sizable sleek rat. This rodent was extraordinarily quick and slippery. He had vast experience with cats and ships. He knew every trick in the book and where there would be a hiding place on any boat, so he gave Licorice and Black Jack a chase every day.

Finally, he was the only rat left aboard; all others had gone to rodent heaven. The cats were at their wit's end. Just when they thought they had the cagey fugitive cornered, he found another crevice through which to dash and slither away.

Black Jack was especially furious. Since his awful experience of trying to catch another rat, when his tail was crushed in two by a grappling hook and bent forever, he never forgot that and swore vengeance on all rats in existence. The cat patrolled the decks and hold day and night, seeking to catch the fat fellow. He lost so much sleep and weight he even forgot to eat when the sailors ate.

Licorice was fearful for his brother. Black Jack was a nervous wreck. Licorice tried purring and wrapping his body around his brother. Licorice could not appease his brother. The only thing Black Jack wanted was to do was to destroy his enemy, the rat.

Both cats knew a living rodent on their ship was not a good thing. They had their reputations to uphold as being the best ratters on the entire seven seas. They were not going to let one rat spoil that!

Up and down, in and out, the cats chased the elusive one, to no avail. The rat tore the bags in the cargo hold to pieces and ate whatever the rodent wanted. It was as though the vermin was daring capture. The destruction was indescribable. The sailors were very unhappy, for a ruined cargo would not bring them money when they tried selling it. No one wanted to eat anything a rodent had traipsed through!

One evening, black clouds gathered, the entire sky turned purple, the wind blew, shrieked furiously, and shredded the hemp sails to tatters. The ship tossed off course violently, and the brothers had to seek shelter below for fear of being swept away. The waves were thirty feet tall, and the ship tilted to such an extreme angle; all hands thought they were lost. The steering became impossible, so the vessel floundered on its own. Every sailor prayed for deliverance from the storm.

Finally, after the boat dashed against huge rocks near a shore, the storm subsided at daybreak. The crew discovered they were near a big city. Their sails were in tatters, and there was a large hole in the ship's port side. The boat needed steering toward the shore to make repairs. The treacherous rat was hiding and peeping out from under one of the lifeboats on the deck. Once the ship docked and dropped anchor and their gangplank, the fat rat took the opportunity to escape. It dashed off down the gangway like a lead ball fired from a blunderbuss.

Black Jack was sitting at the top of the rigging, searching for the rat. He dashed down, zip, and he chased the rodent. Immediately his brother, Licorice, followed. Never once did either cat give a thought; they were once again placing themselves in harm's way by going ashore.

The faster they raced, the quicker the rat fled, through crooked streets, over cobblestones, past garbage, through a fat lady's legs, making her scream to high heaven. She fell with a plop all the food in her cart was scattered everywhere. They chased the rat over and under peddler's carts, spilling apples, oranges, grapes, dry goods all over the narrow streets. They had become like streaks of lightning zip, zip, zip, never stopping for a breath, round and round they went.

By trade, a passing rat catcher, Phineas, tried cornering and corralling the rat, but the rodent was too fast for him. The cats tripped the man; he tumbled to the ground rolling several feet until prevented from rotating any further by a wagon in the street. Licorice and Black Jack never looked back. On and on, they ran.

At last, the rat saw an open door and dashed through. The lady who lived there did not see the rodent enter and closed the door before the cats could follow. Much howling and hissing ensued. They were desolate, for they had lost their prey. They sat before the door, hoping the rat would exit again. No such luck; he stayed safely inside the house.

Licorice and Black Jack looked around bewildered. They realized the city was vast, and they were lost. Where was their ship? Several dirty boys were playing in the street, and they proceeded to throw sticks at the cats; they hit Licorice and hurt him. Both cats took off before the children did any more harm to them. What to do now? Where are we? How can we get back to the ship?

Phineas caught up with the brothers. The rat catcher wore a stovepipe hat and a torn velvet coat he had purloined a month before at a trash heap. The man resembled a rat. He was small, stooped over, and had a pinched face with a short red bulbous nose. Phineas' eyes set close together, and his teeth protruded and extended above his lower lip precisely like the rodents he caught for a living.

With a net, he trapped them both. He threw them in a burlap sack and tossed them over his shoulders. The rat-catcher was ecstatic to have these cats. Phineas decided he would teach them to snag more rats than he could do with his net. People would only pay for a proven catch, and with two cats, he would have the ability to double the money he made before. He once had a rat terrier, but the dog took off several months ago, leaving him with his empty cages and no one to rustle up and route out the rats.

Phineas thought owning the cats might do the trick for him. He knew people paid good wages when he caught a rat. Most people did not try capturing them for fear of being bitten. No one wanted vermin in their house either, but keeping a house rat or mouse free was a challenge and a costly business to the homeowner. He was on call all the time, for it was a massive port city and many ships arrived daily disembarking several rodents with each docking. There was a never-ending supply of rats. His business was thriving, but he could always do more with help.

He lugged the cats to his hovel, plopped the bag down that held them, and barred the door so they could not escape. He dug out an old rusty cage from his root cellar, which he used to collect an overflow of rats, opened the bag, and roughly shoved them in the enclosure, slamming the door. On the bottom of it was a rag with padding of some kind. The container was filthy beyond description. It had chicken wire all around it, making it impossible for the boys to use their other trick with the mutton fat. It looked as though they were there for the long haul and in deeper trouble than before.

"There," he said, "now I'll get something to eat and tend to these rascals later." He went into the kitchen, leaving Licorice and Black Jack in complete befuddlement.

"Lordy, lordy," said Licorice, "we are in the same kind of mess again, tell me we don't have to deal with this once more!"

Black Jack just looked around dolefully and realized that action before thought was dangerous for a cat's existence. Had they pondered their situation and not chased that danged ding rat, they would not be in this fix, and they would still be aboard their beloved ship with their shipmates.

Phineas had an off-and-on girlfriend who was shady like him. She was fat, with greasy hair. Her clothes were never clean. She wore the same skirt day in and day out. She wore a colored bandanna and huge gold earrings. Her family had been gypsies, but they had moved on when she was little—leaving her to fend for herself. She transacted many unsavory dealings to earn a living. Cassiopeia read Tarot cards for clients and was quite good at it. She would visit him to practice her ability with the cards as often as he would put up with it. She called it "honing her skills."

The very night Phineas caught the cats, she decided to visit. She sashayed into the hovel with a bag of cards and a bottle of cheap wine. Cassiopeia loved cats and asked Phineas to give them to her as pets. He laughed at her and said, "these are going to be my money-making meal tickets."

He was not glad to see Cassiopeia but was delighted to see the wine. She was disappointed with his refusal but still was going to share her wine with him. Cassiopeia got two dirty glasses out of the dishpan, dropped down at the table, opened the wine, poured each of them a drink, and spread her Tarot cards out for display.

While Cassiopea practiced with her cards, the cats were crouched, peering at her from their cage over her shoulder. They were intensely watching her every move. After a while, they got the sense of how to predict a person's future. She stayed way into the night, casting hand after hand. The boys observed her every move. When the wine was gone, Phineas ushered Cassiopeia out, he'd had enough of her foolishness for one day, and she was of little use to him once the wine was gone.

In any case, Phineas outfitted both boys with pronged choke collars with metal studs; when the cats would restrain against them, it would bite into their necks and chew their fur. They quickly learned not to fight it. Phineas started teaching the cats about walking around town to sniff out rodents, and after meeting a client, the ratter let them off their leashes to hunt rats. Once they did the job, it was back on the chain again. He would only let one off at a time, for he knew they were close, and one would not leave without the other.

In the meantime, the shipmates and the Captain did all they could to discover the cats' whereabouts. Finally, once again, they posted wanted ads around the town. They distributed them at every boat dock, purser's mate, and with every Captain that came into port. Once again, the reward was 1,000 doubloons. A nice sum for anyone! Fortunately, the ship was dry-docked due to severe damage and would be required to remain in port for several months before they could sail again, and they were going to have adequate time to search for Licorice and Black Jack and maybe find them.

While scratching the bottom of their pen to sharpen their nails, Licorice and Black Jack discovered the padding on the bottom of their crate was old Tarot cards. The cats began to practice the way they saw Cassiopeia do. After a while, it became less complicated for them to read the cards. Each time they practiced; they covered them up with the old greasy rag that covered the crate's bottom again.

It was their only entertainment source, and they did not want it taken away from them. They could not imagine what good it would do to have this skill, but it helped them pass the time while hoping they could find a means of escape. One day, Cassiopeia caught the cats playing with the Tarot cards; she kept the secret from Phineas. She knew he would find a way to monopolize it. He was so greedy and selfish, she thought.

Every time Cassiopeia visited, she would bring Licorice and Black Jack fresh salmon. She loved the cats and still wanted them for herself. She knew Phineas would not change his mind, so just seeing them was the next best thing. The cats became fond of Cassiopeia and looked forward to her visits. She would always ask Phineas to open their cage and let her pet them. Several times he allowed her to do so.

Several months after their captivity, Cassiopeia visited with a half-gallon of wine. Phineas was delighted. They sat down at the table, she with her cards, and he with the wine. After a while, he got mellow, and she said to him, "We have been seeing each other for three years, don't you think it's time for us to marry?"

Phineas reared back in his chair and laughed until tears ran down his face. "Marry you? You're only good for one thing, and that's to bring wine. You're fat, ugly, and dirty; why would I want to marry you? Nobody in their right mind would either. You just need a burlap sack over your head. Are you crazy?"

Cassiopeia began to cry. How crushed she felt! Phineas looked at her and laughed while he drank the last of the wine. At that point Cassiopeia became irate! "I have been seeing you all these years, and you never refused my visits or my wine. I thought we had a serious relationship. Now, after all this time, you refuse to marry me and call me names?"

Phineas again said, "not going to happen. I once had a wife who ran off with another man and took all my money, not making that mistake twice."

Cassiopeia was so angry she bopped Phineas on the head with the empty wine bottle. He staggered, fell, hit his head on the table, and was out like a light. Cassiopeia reached up, opened the cage, and let the cats out. She grabbed her Tarot cards bag and unlocked the front door, and off they went. She knew if he awoke and she was there, he would call the police for her having hit him, and she would probably have to go to jail.

As soon as they were around the corner, she removed their horrible collars and tossed them out of sight. She did not feel guilty because she thought he was selfish and always taking and never giving in return. Serves him right, she thought.

A traveling carnival was in town. It was the highlight of the year. Annually the show came and stayed for four weeks. They had elephants, giraffes, bears, lions, tigers, monkeys, high wire acts, tumblers, and clowns galore. It was something everyone wanted to experience at least once in their lifetime. All year long, folks saved up their pennies to do just that.

The carnival owner's name was Barclay. He made vast sums of money when his acts were in town, but since it was the same year after year, fewer people came because they saw all there was. He was concerned as his intake dwindled because it cost a great deal to feed all the animals and pay the carnival workers.

The cats and Cassiopeia racing around spotted the carnival lights and wagons. Not knowing when Phineas would discover them missing, they wanted to hide as quickly as possible. The pint-sized rat-catcher could be vicious, and Cassiopeia hitting him and taking his cats would be a bit much for him.

Seeing a wagon, they decided it would be an excellent place in which to hide. The cats jumped up on the wagon and hid under a blanket on a cot. Seeing they were safely out of sight for the moment, Cassiopeia went around the carnival grounds seeking the owner or the head ringmaster. She decided she wanted to leave town, and maybe she could land a job with the carnival reading Tarot cards.

Finally, she found Mr. Barclay, and they discussed her talents. He was excited about it, especially when she told him she had two cats that were part of her act that could read Tarot cards too!

Mr. Barclay said, "you have to show me that for me to believe such a thing."

They went back to the wagon where Licorice and Black Jack were hiding, lit a lantern, and after Cassiopeia called them out, she had them do their thing! They pulled each card for her and set up the arrangement for reading. Licorice and Black Jack tapped each card, and she proceeded to tell Mr. Barclay's fortune. He was astonished. What? Tarot reading cats, no one has ever heard of such a thing. What a stellar act this is going to be. This stunt is fantastic!

The carnival was leaving in a few days, they would have time to practice, and they would have a new act to present to the next town's audience. He hired Cassiopeia immediately and gave her his best wagon in which to live. Having been rescued from Phineas' grasp, the cats were immensely grateful and decided not to run away for a while; they would stay with Cassiopeia and help her make a living.

Mr. Barclay billed Cassiopeia, Licorice, and Black Jack as "Madame Cassiopeia's Mystical Tarot Reading Cats from the Orient." Licorice and Black Jack were the stellar attractions people came from far and wide to see them. The lines were so long Mr. Barclay had to sell advance tickets daily, and there was never a time when no people were waiting to look at the cats and Cassiopeia.

Licorice and Black Jack became a favorite of all the carney people they were fed and petted by all. They charmed every roustabout and carnival hand. No matter how hardened they were, the cats were able to warm everyone's heart. They chased the mice away, which made folks happy, for the rodents were always around, what with people dropping bits of candy apples and popcorn all over the fairgrounds.

The big fat four-hundred-pound lady with the beard and mustache loved them more than anyone else. When the carnival shut down each evening, she sat with them in her cozy lap for hours as they slept and purred the night away, dreaming of the open seas.

Two monkeys were part of an act at the carnival. Their names were Moe and Slick. They rode ponies, did somersault tricks, and jumped through hoops while the miniature horses circled round and round a ring. Mr. Barclay had initially bought a family of six lemurs. These primates were rare and came from the island of Columbar.

The monkeys had black and white faces, brown bodies, and long black and white ringed tails. Having huge round eyes like saucers made one think they were full of curiosity. When he purchased them, the carnival owner thought they would make an excellent addition to his extravaganza.

Barclay did not know that four of the troop were very sick and died within two weeks of acquiring them. The remaining two were enormously depressed after the rest of their family passed away and would do nothing but sit in their cage with their heads down. They moped all day long. The carnival owner was worried about them, but he did not know what to do about it. He found out they loved sugar, so he would give them something sweet daily to keep their spirits up. They especially liked the cotton candy, but it would get matted in their hair, so he rarely gave him that treat. Mr. Barclay was upset, he had planned to have a spectacular act, but due to their mournful behavior, that probably would not be possible.

After the Licorice and Black Jack arrived, the monkeys roused themselves. They were curious about these new animals. Mr. Barclay discovered Moe and Slick appeared to like Licorice and Black Jack. He opened their cage to see what would happen once the cats and monkeys met face to face. The apes immediately jumped on the cat's backs and rode with arms wrapped around their necks with great joy.

To everyone's surprise, this became an act in itself. So, between Tarot reading and their riding show, the monkeys and cats were not only famous but extremely busy. Too busy to get into any trouble, as was their habit of doing.

One day Cassiopeia caught the cats teaching Moe and Slick to read the Tarot cards. Licorice and Black Jack thought if the monkeys became proficient, they could leave Cassiopeia, not feeling they had betrayed her. After all, they knew they probably would not have had a decent, happy life with Phineas. He had expected them to hunt from morning to night, then back in the cage with them until the next day's foray! They wanted to show their gratitude, but they also needed to find their ship and be on their way. They missed the sea terribly.

The lemurs were highly intelligent and learned rapidly, as a matter of fact, faster than Licorice and Black Jack had. Each cat practiced patience and Moe, and Slick took to the skill like ducks to water. Cassiopeia was not too happy about the monkeys learning her act, for she was afraid it would become standard practice and reduce her show's popularity at the carnival.

Living with the carnival folk was the first time Cassiopeia had felt respected. She certainly did not want to lose her new station in life. She also had the companionship of Barclay. She did not want him to tire of her.

Once Licorice and Black Jack realized that Cassiopeia was upset about it, they taught the monkeys secretly when the gypsy was not around. She never once thought the cats would leave her, but she didn't want to lose her stellar position at the carnival.

Mr. Barclay took a fancy to Cassiopeia and brought her flowers and candy regularly. They played cards and drank wine occasionally and laughed many a night until daybreak. Cassiopeia realized she had a new beau; began to dress carefully, curled her hair, got rid of her greasy bandanna, and regularly used the outside shower. She became quite the looker. Many a carnival hand admired her, but she had eyes only for Barclay.

A small passing caravan wagon stopped by the carnival. It was ragged, old, dirty, and in a state of disrepair. It contained a family of gypsies distantly related to Cassiopeia. She was joyful to see them again. She got all the family news. They were even more thrilled because she had risen so high in the carnival world. They thought they could sweet-talk her out some money or into helping them join the carnival.

Cassiopeia wasn't that naïve. She knew a con when she saw one. When they realized she was on to them, they became furious. Madame, indeed, how about that, she's no better than us, she came from the same roots! Now she thinks she's something special.

Soon it became evident to Cassiopeia that her long-lost family were just scam artists and wanted everything from her and were not planning on giving anything back.

Finally, she gave them the cold shoulder and told them they had to move on, for she could not afford to support them, herself, and her cats. They eyed the cats with envy, they thought, how dare she have so much, and we have so little. She must think she is better than us. We'll show her. How good will she be when her cats are lost?

One night when it was pitch black, the down at the heels family crept up to Cassiopeia's wagon. As luck would have it for them, they discovered she was visiting Mr. Barclay's cart that evening. They snatched the cats rudely by the scruff of their necks, slammed them into a bag, and stole away into the night.

When Cassiopeia returned, it was dark, and she thought Licorice and Black Jack were with the fat lady, so she dropped off to sleep like a rock and slept the night away dreaming of Barclay and the wonderful time they were having. When she woke up, the cats were gone, so were her slippery relatives. Oh, heavens, what now?

No more Tarot Playing cats, all is lost. She was walking about wringing her hands when she saw Moe and Slick reading someone's future. That gave her an idea she would use the monkeys instead of the cats. She certainly would miss the little fellows, though. She had no idea her worthless family had snatched them. She just thought they had tired of carnival life and ran off. Cassiopeia was not angry because they had taught the little lemurs to become Tarot readers.

Phineas woke slowly. He did not remember what happened. He had a substantial purple egg on his forehead, an empty bottle of wine, an open cage, and no cats. Cassiopeia was gone. After thinking it over, all the past events returned to his memory. "Good riddance to her, I'll miss the wine, but I want my cats back."

He got himself together and searched the streets for them after going to her room and finding her missing. She was not there, nowhere. It looked as though she left in a hurry, for most of her raggedy stuff was still there!

Dagnabbit, no cats, no wine, what's a man to do? That thief, what an ingrate, after all the time I spent in her company, ungrateful little wretch!

Phineas searched for Licorice and Black Jack for several days, losing a lot of money due to failing to catch rats. Finally, he had to give up the hunt and get back to ratting in earnest, or he would not be able to pay any of his bills. Phineas would then go to the debtor's prison and starve if that happened. The rat catcher had no family to pay his debts and bail him out. He was a miserable man.

The traveling gypsies were not very smart. They placed Licorice and Black Jack in a box without any restraints on it. The cats nestled in it, awaiting an excellent time to make their escape. They made no noise for fear the thieves would realize their error and place them in a more secure holding pen.

A lame youngster begging for coins was sitting on the street when a sailor passed. The seaman wanted to go to the carnival. He asked the lad where it was. The boy told him its location and related the great news about the two black Tarot reading cats. The sailor was amazed; could it be Licorice and Black Jack? Those two cats are smart enough to do anything. I'll bet my bell-bottoms it is them!

He thanked the lad and dashed off in the direction of the carnival. When he got there, he asked a roustabout where he could find the cats. The man told him they belonged to Cassiopeia and where her wagon was, but alas, when he located it and spoke to her, she said some worthless family members of hers stole them and had runoff. The seaman asked how long they'd been gone. Cassiopeia said she did not know. However, when she returned last night, they were already gone. He thanked her and took off rapidly down the road out of town.

As luck would have it, the wagon wheel in which the gypsy family was traveling fell off, and the travelers became stuck in a muddy rut. They were lamenting their misfortune when the sailor came along. He, at first, offered to help them remount the wheel when he heard meowing from the back of the wagon.

When Licorice and Black Jack recognized their friend's voice, they leaped out of the box and into his arms. He told the travelers he would call the sheriff if they had any trouble with him taking the cats. They knew they had stolen them and could say nothing. The sailor left them without helping to repair their wheel. He took off for the ship as quickly as he could.

The ship's crew had repaired the hole in the port side of the boat. The Fair Winds was sailing from port to port, trying to pick up extra cargo to make up for the lost time. Fortunately, Licorice and Black Jack's vessel had just arrived on shore, and the ship was going to spend several days in port to load cargo. Once the sailor boarded the boat, he reported to the Captain, with Licorice and Black Jack wrapped securely in his arms. The Captain could not believe his eyes. He had his beloved cats once again.

The seaman told of the lame beggar boy and said he gave him information to find the cats. The Captain opened the ship's safe and placed the 1,000 doubloons in a leather pouch. He asked the seaman to locate the youngster and give him the reward.

The young seaman took off with the money and found the little boy. He gave him the money, and the youngster had tears in his eyes. He said his mother was extremely sick, and they were about to be dispossessed and homeless. Now with the money, all would be well again. He thanked the seaman and limped off home to tell his mother the fantastic news.

Meanwhile, Barclay had just received a letter from a barrister in Africa that a distant uncle had died and left him a vast banana plantation on the island of Columbar. Barclay was so happy he almost cried. The carnival owner was sorry for his uncle's loss but delighted to be the inheritor of a banana farm. He immediately went to Cassiopeia and asked her to marry him. She said yes before he could finish the sentence. There was a traveling preacher with the carnival that married them right away.

The next day Mr. Barclay and Cassiopeia went to the land office and offered his entire carnival, except the lemurs for sale. A gentleman who was in town was interested, and they came to a rapid agreement. That settled, they went to the docks in search of a boat to book passage to Columbar.

The ship sailing directly for the Dark Continent was the boat on which Licorice and Black Jack lived. What a grand surprise. After shopping for new duds, both Mr. Barclay and Cassiopeia were happy to leave carnival life.

At the end of a week, they boarded the boat. Licorice and Black Jack were delighted to see Moe and Slick too. The monkeys were happy that they would be returning to Columbar. They still had a family there and longed to see and be with them. Up went the Fair Winds' sails, the anchor, and off they sailed, never looking back, only forward to new adventures.

Licorice and Black Jack on Columbar Island

Licorice and Black Jack awoke. They were lulled and rocked gently back and forth with the ocean rhythm. Nothing was like being aboard the Fair Winds. They had been everywhere else and tried sleeping, but only when the sweet waves rocked them could they feel entirely at home and safe.

The ship left Rotterdam headed for Columbar Island. It was going to be a long, long voyage. They had to sail all around the West Coast of Africa beneath the Cape of Good Hope and arrive at their destined island sometime later. Never before had they traveled that far. It didn't matter, though, for it was of no consequence. They did not care, only to be with their beloved shipmates, the Captain, and out in the open air was essential to them.

This trip was going to be a maiden voyage for Barclay, Cassiopeia, Moe, and Slick. Even though Moe and Slick's parents were initially from Columbar, these little fellows were born in England. They, like all those aboard, would be seeing that island for the first time. They had a large troop of relatives still living there, and Moe and Slick were looking forward to meeting them for the first time. The troop was born in captivity, so they had a great deal to learn about living free and roaming all over. The thought of jumping from tree to tree intrigued them. There were to be lots of bananas, mangoes, sugar cane, nuts for the taking. There was to be no more waiting to eat. The monkeys could eat when they wanted and as much as they desired, to the bursting point if they took a mind to do so. Yeah!

Mr. Barclay had sold his lucrative carnival property lock, stock, and barrel. He married Cassiopeia, and they would make their home henceforth in Columbar. Mr. Barclay had inherited a banana plantation from a deceased uncle, who was unknown to him. When he was a youngster, he heard mention of an uncle who lived in Africa, but he had to leave the room, or the conversation ended abruptly whenever the subject came up.

Mr. Barclay never wondered about that because children were seen and not heard; it was unheard of questioning adults. In any case, he was an only child, and the inheritance was for him alone. From now on, he and Cassiopeia would have plenty on which to live. They would have no more worries about making ends meet, as was prevalent in carnival life.

The cats were delighted to have Moe and Slick's company as sailors were fun, but they had duties to perform on shipboard and could not play endless, full-time shenanigans and horseplay with them as they would have liked. They were happy Cassiopeia was along for the journey because they loved to cuddle in her lap when she took tea.

Moe and Slick could give a rousing chase up and down the lanyards. Only their long ringed tails were visible. What fun, who would have thought it? Paradise supreme, that is what it was. Chasing, mice, and rats playing endlessly with Moe and Slick, entertaining the sailors, hour upon hour life could not be better. Being able to eat their fill at every mess call was a glorious thing. Nothing could be beyond this bliss!

Loaded to the top of the ship's cargo hold, the Fair Winds sailed effortlessly. If they made a safe voyage, the Captain and all hands would realize a hefty profit. The Captain's name was Benjamin Schiff. There was a lovely lady in Liverpool, England, named Veronica, waiting patiently for his return.

Captain Schiff would ask her to marry him when he returned to England. They had separated for such a long time, but that was the life of a seafaring man. Once they married, he hoped to convince her to sail with him and make her home on the seas in the Fair Winds. Of course, that would have to wait until his crew completed this long, dangerous trip.

Several times they saw other vessels passing in the opposite direction from them. They hoisted their flags in recognition of them, but none requested to come aboard. Captain Schiff was grateful for that because any delay would prolong his voyage and return to the lovely Veronica.

These were dangerous times; it was the age of the slave trade. Most of the ships going to Africa carried cargo and staples. On their return from the continent, the vessels held human cargo. There was stiff competition between countries, ship owners, and their captains. The desired results were to capture as many slaves as possible and pack them in their boats' hull. The more slaves they acquired, the more likely many would survive the arduous, dreadful, dangerous trip. The African natives were referred to as Black Gold, among other vile names used to describe them.

Once the ship arrived at its intended destination, the slaves were unloaded and placed in slave forts to await an auction. These venues were known as "Table Vendue." If the chattel became ill and died, there would be no profit. Knowing this did nothing to make the owners treat the slaves humanely to assure their safe arrival.

The Captain ordered dead slaves thrown overboard the ships. If a captive became ill or in any way thwarted the will of the masters, they were ejected from the boat to discourage others from attempting the same behavior. These corpses floated past the Fair Winds, sometimes bumping into the sides, making weird, eerie noises.

Cassiopeia would turn her head and cry when she saw this poor sight bob pass. She would lock herself up in her cabin and be distraught for hours on end. Nature has a way of handling its leavings. In this case, the sharks were always around circling the boats of slaves and the discarded bodies. They were always available to make short work of the poor souls who died in this manner.

Captain Schiff was not in favor of slavery but unable to do anything about it except refuse to handle such cargo. Africa was a massive country, travel was slow, and only so many nautical knots could be traversed daily. The Fair Winds would dock around the coast occasionally to take on fresh fruit, water, and provisions. They would anchor up as rapidly as possible, as Captain Schiff did not want to stay any significant time where open slave markets and active auctions were.

When the Fair Winds did dock, the shipboard company could evidence the slave's abuse. They were pushed, prodded with cattle prods, poked, humiliated, and beaten into submission on the vendor's block. The thought of slavery was terrible, but the actual visual of the misery was beyond comprehension. Little children separated from their parents, mothers, and fathers separated from each other, never in contact again. They were sold to different captains on different ships, going in opposite directions, torn apart, what ghastly misery!

Licorice and Black Jack had no idea what was happening, but they could sense something was casting a pall over the entire ship once it hit the African Coast. The sailors were quiet, no rousing singing or dancing, and no tall tales, only work and dour looks. Nothing cheered the crew.

Licorice and Black Jack tried performing their usual antics, but they were to no avail. The cats were at their wits end! Moe and Slick did no chattering, no skittering, just sad little monkey faces with droopy ringed tails.

The purpose of the Fair Winds' trip to Columbar was to off-load their cargo of staples and provisions, and then they were to pick up precious gemstones from a man who owned two large mines of rubies and sapphires. The jewels of Columbar were world-renown, and everyone wanted something fabricated of them. They would then sail to Amsterdam to a famous jeweler who made one-of-a-kind masterpieces for the royalty of Europe.

After that, they would be paid and once again depart for Liverpool, England, their home port. Captain Schiff thought this was going to be a simple voyage with significant financial gain for all. He also had the princely sum of money paid by Cassiopeia and Barclay for their berth. This trip should make him financially secure to ask for Veronica's hand in marriage.

Usually, Licorice and Black Jack were very cool customers. The only thing that could bother them would have to deal with a rampant rat problem. If anyone bothered the other, this could get them riled up a few notches, but this "slavery thing" was another story; it was way over the top. The brothers realized this was not the way they usually lived. They did not understand it one iota.

They were accustomed to happy frolicsome times, foolishness, and rowdy fun. Not this insane situation that they now were observing. This situation was similar to being kidnapped by Klutz and being caged and mistreated by Phineas and made to wear notched collars. The only redeeming characteristic was they were never parted from each other. They had immense sympathy for those torn apart from family members. They realized their treatment was nothing like these poor souls were being subject to, but it was the only comparison they could make of the current situation.

Life should be full of fun and joy, not this. Why on Earth is this happening? What could make one treat another this way? It was not so in the animal kingdom. Each beast had a purpose, live and let live unless it was for survival. One had to hunt or become the hunted; that was the natural way of life. It was not about enslaving a creature and making them lose their will to live and their dignity. What an impossible situation.

Since they were unable to communicate with the crew, they just became more gloomy and quiet. The situation affected the sailors, they knew the cats were usually up to hi-jinks, and they could not figure out the trouble. They were afraid the cats had caught an illness, and they had no medicine or professional help for them. The ship's doctor knew a lot about healing men but did not know cats or their sicknesses.

The seamen also noted the further away the felines were from any passing vessel, the happier they appeared to be. They, too, were upset about the passing slave ships but not as much as it affected the brothers. The Fair Winds out of Liverpool, England, flew the British flag. She met many a boat that hoisted myriad flags from all over the world. The Fair Winds was a cargo ship with a capacity for a few first-class passengers.

Since the Fair Winds carried no valuables to other vessel's knowledge, they were not attacked or stopped by pirates or brigands. They usually had safe passage wherever they sailed.

These people who were being corralled and made slaves of were black like Licorice and Black Jack. Being black never mattered to the cats. At least they did not think they were hated any worse than any other cat. Being solid black had its advantage. They were unusual and thought of as beautiful and exotic. They had seen a few men of color, brown, yellow, and black, in their travels.

Never had they observed so many black folks in such immense numbers as they saw now. They never envisioned there were so many other people of color in the world. They never thought about it until now. Astounding, they thought, people come in all shapes, sizes, and colors.

What a surprise. Licorice and Black Jack wondered what the people were like and precisely from where they came. They also pondered what they had done for such horrible treatment. Usually, people treated each other poorly when they had committed a crime or done some heinous act. Could it be that even little children were criminals?

In England, the cats knew there was a debtor's prison. When one didn't pay their obligations, the Crown tossed you into a drafty cell and threw away the key. If they could discharge their fines, they would obtain their freedom. If they didn't have the money to pay, others might defray their costs, and the debtor would be indentured to the payee for a certain number of years depending on the price of what was due by physically working off the debt by indentured service.

The slaves' problem didn't appear to be the same kind of situation. Was there nothing the black creatures could do to save themselves? Why on Earth was this happening, the cats pondered? If this was what growing up was all about, they didn't want any part of it. Was there no way out for these people? Could nothing be done to stop this? Was being black a crime in itself?

Finally, after tumultuous tossing and dashing around the "Horn" they sailed smoothly to the shores of Columbar. They breathed many a sigh of relief. The "Horn" was a scary place to navigate, and many a ship met their end while sailing there.

Everyone landed and tried practicing walking steadily. Barclay and Cassiopeia had already packed their sea trunks. They off-loaded their entire luggage with the help of the seamen. Once on the dock, all the baggage was placed in a horse-drawn wagon. They asked the townspeople for directions to the livery stable, for they wanted to hire a cart driver. Once they found a suitable driver, who knew how to navigate to the banana plantation, they hired him on the spot.

The Captain asked Barclay and Cassiopeia if they would look after Licorice and Black Jack until he could come for them. Captain Schiff wanted to oversee the ship's off-loading and assure that supplies got to the intended vendors. The Captain also wanted to visit the ruby and sapphire mines owner to obtain the precious gems for transportation to the Amsterdam jeweler. He did not want to drag the cats around, for he did not know how long the negotiations would take. Nor did he want them to take off again on some crazy adventure, meaning he would have to search for them once more. Enough was enough, and he was sure if they stayed with the Barclay's, they would be safe.

Barclay and Cassiopeia were delighted to have the cat brothers accompany them as they could keep Moe and Slick company. As the cats were sad during the trip, they wanted to change the scenery for them for a while. Off they drove, in the direction of the banana plantation.

Moe and Slick chattering away, racing back and forth in the wagon, driving the livery driver and the horses crazy, with their herky-jerky movements. The monkeys were in a state of agitation and anticipation about seeing their distant family. The massive excitement was everywhere. Barclay and Cassiopeia were looking forward to a new life, and the monkeys were anxious for an unfettered life of complete freedom.

Just before nightfall, the party arrived at the plantation. It was too dark to see the surrounding area. Mr. Barclay paid the driver handsomely, and he departed after he unloaded all the gear. Subdued servants greeted Barclay and Cassiopeia immediately. They were standing outside of the mansion at strict attention on either side of the long, winding walkway. They carried the baggage into the house. What a villa! Barclay and Cassiopeia could not believe their eyes.

The monkeys and cats jumped down from the wagon and began investigating the entire property within. There was no controlling them, so Barclay let them have at it.

The couple was astounded. It was a massive mansion. The property was nothing like Barclay and Cassiopeia had ever expected. It was way beyond their wildest dreams! What a surprise! They were shown up a grand circular staircase to a lovely bedroom after being escorted through a long hallway with six or seven rooms on either side of it.

The house was furnished magnificently with rich damask drapery, oriental carpets covered the teak floors, and valuable antiques were everywhere. This was a house fit for royalty, not for a carnival owner and a gypsy Tarot reader. 'Well,' thought Barclay, 'I and my lady love will make sure we get used to it. Go figure, how life does you a turn. You never know; you're on your lowers one day, and then the next, you're at the top of the world.' It was almost impossible to believe such riches, but here they were, whew!

Everything was shiny, clean, and polished to a golden sheen. Barclay and Cassiopeia noticed that the silver items on the dining room sideboard shone and sparkled as they passed. There wasn't a dust mote anywhere.

Barclay and Cassiopeia were exhausted from their long and arduous trip, so after being served a light supper of fruit and soup, they told the servants they were going to bed. They asked the servants to feed Licorice, Black Jack, Moe, and Slick and asked them to take care of the animals for them. The servants were eager to please and corralled the animals into the kitchen and fed them as requested.

While Barclay and Cassiopeia were sleeping, Licorice and Black Jack prowled the area. They discovered lots of straw huts with black people enchained within. The cabins had dirt floors, only one entrance, and a hole in the top of the thatch work roof to emit smoke from cooking. There were no windows to circulate the air. Africa is very hot during the day but can be intensely cold at night. The slaves tried to keep warm but had little to cover them and only had the bare, dirt floors on which to sleep. Their condition was dire.

The one large center building housed the overseers. It had a proper front and back, windows, and a brick chimney to emit the cooking smoke. They also had beds within for each overseer and separate rooms with doors to provide privacy for them. It appeared they suffered minimal discomfort. The cats prowled unnoticed as they were black, and who pays attention to a cat? Nobody, that's who, Licorice and Black Jack got a good idea of the lay of the land.

The quiet was deafening. Each slave was trying to sleep as best as possible, for they knew dawn was rapidly approaching, and they would have to work in the sugar cane fields, the banana/mango trees, the rice paddies, or worse yet, the cotton fields.

While Licorice and Black Jack were on their productive prowl, Moe and Slick slept like babies on a silk pillow at the foot of the bed in Barclay and Cassiopeia's room. What luxury. Even Cassiopeia's carnival wagon did not provide such luxury as this! 'We've died and gone to heaven,' the monkeys thought.

The following day came quickly, too quickly for Barclay and Cassiopeia. Once they were awake, they heard gentle knocking on their bedroom door—Cassiopeia bid whoever was there to come in. Several servants entered carrying a colossal pitcher of warm water to wash and fluffy towels to dry afterward. Barclay and Cassiopeia said, "we could get used to this fast."

After washing and dressing, a servant said Mr. Tweed, the barrister for Barclay's uncle's estate, was waiting in the library to see them. Barclay looked for the library. The house was so immense, they were afraid they would get lost, and he didn't have the vaguest idea of its location.

One of the servants led him to it, and once they entered, they discovered books everywhere on shelves from the ceiling to the floor. Shelves and shelves of beautiful leather-bound first edition books! Good Lord, Barclay thought, my uncle must have been a millionaire. Go figure, my family never told me about him or his circumstances, just that he was his father's brother.

The barrister, Mr. Tweed, who resembled a giant egg, had a few sprigs of light brown hair poking from the top of his head, square spectacles, and a potbelly with short bow legs. He wore a bright-colored brocade vest and a big bow tie as if to give himself an air of respectability. What a sight! He had a fawning manner and humbly greeted them by bowing deeply.

Both Cassiopeia and Barclay thought he was going to topple over due to such deep bowing. How embarrassed Barclay was for him but tried not showing how he felt. On the other hand, Cassiopeia had to place her handkerchief in front of her mouth to keep from snickering.

The servants brought refreshments and left immediately. After introductions were complete, Mr. Tweed reached into his brown leather bag, pulled out Barclay's uncle's will, and began to read it officiously.

"You have inherited 150 acres of mango and 150 acres of banana trees, you also have 150 acres of sugar cane, 150 acres of cotton, and finally, last but not least, you own 50 acres of rice paddies. The total acreage comes to 650 acres. You have a massive paddock of seventy-five purebred horses and hundreds of longhorn cattle, a multitude of sheep, and an innumerable flock of poultry. The plantation is enormous, whose annual yield is tremendous. It is self-sustaining and provides much produce for the ships that sail here in search of provisions."

"Great land, a Goshen! Now, what do you think of that?"

Barclay kept mulling this massive number over and over in his head. Cassiopeia just stared wide-eyed and tried to keep her mouth from gaping open! She was rapidly fanning herself with her lacey handkerchief to prevent from having the vapors and passing out with shock. Then she thought, 'no gypsy ever fainted, I must get hold of myself, really, I do believe that I am beginning to put on airs! That has to stop here and now, Lordy, me.'

At that point, Mr. Tweed stuck out what little chest he had; actually, it was his rotund belly and said something with a subservient manner; "you also have five-hundred field slaves and twenty house slaves. You employ six overseers, one for each field and one to look over the house servants. You, Mr. Barclay, are an immensely wealthy man. If I may be of further service, do not hesitate to send for me day or night." Being paid a generous salary, he wanted that income to continue for as long as possible.

Immediately without one word but a quick look and a silent nod at each other, in unison, they asked Mr. Tweed to provide them, that very day, with all records and account books about the management of the plantation. Mr. Tweed complied and said he was returning to town as he had an urgent meeting with some bankers, but if they sent one of the house slaves to accompany him, he would give the servant the books right away. The slave was provided with a horse and rode off, following Mr. Tweed to fetch the papers.

Once the barrister left, Barclay sat there with his mouth open, and he could hardly breathe. Cassiopeia, like her husband, was astonished and could not utter one word. Her eyes bugged, and she just sat there in her oversized chair in utter befuddlement, fanning herself more and more briskly and becoming hotter in doing so.

Finally, Barclay found the words to say it is one thing to have all this wealth, indeed excellent, but altogether another to have it derived from owning human beings. We have to rectify that as soon as we understand our situation. Cassiopeia said she wholeheartedly agreed.

Meanwhile, Moe and Slick had slipped out of the house and took off to find their long-lost family members. A wagon full of kegs of water was passing. It was going in the direction of the mountains where their family lived. The monkeys quietly hitched a ride. Better riding than loping along, they thought. The wagon driver did not suspect he had hitchhikers with him.

Licorice and Black Jack had a good look at the situation and were utterly disgusted with what that look revealed. Other than the house slaves, who were consistently in silent fear of doing something wrong, having their status changed, or in fear of being sold to some other plantation owner, they were not beaten and were fed well with the residue in the kitchen.

Worry was a constant that loomed like smoke overhead day and night. The house slaves were allowed to bathe once a week. The females wore headscarves to keep a stray strand of hair out of the food. They dressed adequately, not in finery, but modestly covered.

The field slaves wore rags and given only one change of clothing annually to celebrate Christmas. They came from primarily Muslim countries, knew nothing of, nor did they celebrate the birth of Christ. They had no idea about what the celebration was. They only knew they got new hemp clothes to wear once a year. Their old clothes were put on a huge bonfire and burned up Christmas evening.

On Christmas day, they were allowed to march down to the ocean and bathe themselves before putting on their new burlap sacks. One full day of rest was allowed. The families could get together and sing and pray. However, most of them could not converse, for the tribes at the plantation spoke many dialects of African.

Few could communicate with others as they were from the different tribes of Africa and had no knowledge of each other's language. Lack of communication was the way slave owners controlled their chattel. Since they could not talk with each other, read, or write, the possibility of an uprising was remote.

When many African tribes were free, they ate no pork because their religion forbade it. Once they became captives of the slave owners, they had to eat the leftovers of pigs, i.e., chitterlings, pig's tails, pig's feet, entrails of pigs, and sometimes offered an occasional pig head. The owners ate the hams, ribs, bacon, and chops of the pork.

Slave owners forced their captives to go against their religious beliefs and eat whatever was thrown at them to stay alive. Daily they were beaten, kicked, and physically mistreated in every way, at the caprice of the overseers. They wore iron manacles on their necks, wrists, and ankles. These shackles were continually rubbing against their skin and making them chafe, which kept the surrounding flesh with never-healing open and infected sores.

The slaves arose at dawn, given little to eat; what they got was worse than the hogs' slops. They were then walked or driven by cattle prod to their respective work fields for another full day of sheer drudgery. Columbar being an island, provided no escape route. Once a slave was there, it was forever, and most times, a slave was born and died under the whip on that small exotic, beautiful island.

Licorice and Black Jack were overwhelmed with this abysmal horror. They dashed back to the manor house to try to communicate the misery to Barclay and Cassiopeia.

Barclay and Cassiopeia were still unaware of the entire situation. All they knew was they wanted to correct these wrongs. They needed to figure out what needed to be done. They desired to keep the yield from the plantation working and financially stable. Five hundred twenty souls to be responsible for was not desirable to either of them.

The carnival owner thought that his having run a street fair was a challenge. What a hoot, that was a piece of cake in comparison to this arduous task. What on Earth was he thinking? How on Earth will we be able to manage this situation? After Mr. Tweed departed, he pondered this enigma. Just thinking about it was exhausting and mind-boggling.

Licorice and Black Jack skittered into the library, looking frazzled. Barclay and Cassiopeia did, too; even though the cats could not communicate, each knew the other was aghast at the same situation. They just sat in complete silence and stared at one another.

It was time for everyone to eat something, so Cassiopeia rang the bell which hung beside the curtain. A servant hurried in before the signal could stop ringing. Everyone was startled with such rapidity of response. In any case, Cassiopeia requested that they all eat and suggested the meal; they brought it immediately.

Licorice and Black Jack were delighted, fresh fish, what a treat! If the slavery thing were not an issue, this would be paradise on Earth for them. In any case, after eating, Barclay and Cassiopeia retired for an afternoon siesta, and the cats curled up to catch a little snooze also.

Meanwhile, Moe and Slick arrived at the mountainous terrain where their family lived. They hopped off the wagon, unseen by the driver, and rushed to meet their clan. All the monkeys made chattering noises of greeting; everyone appeared to be delighted to see Moe and Slick. In the monkey language, they found out about the death of the family members who had lived and traveled with the carnival. They were sorry to hear about their demise but delighted to know Moe and Slick survived.

The troop formed a circle and chittered about many subjects, mainly about the slavery situation on the island. None of the monkeys had been captive for even a moment. They could not fathom what such an existence as that would be.

Moe and Slick wanted the monkey clan to meet Licorice and Black Jack, because it was due to them, they were free and unfettered. The troop agreed to catch the next wagon or cart going south to meet the cats. That settled; Moe and Slick began to eat bananas; the troop taught them how to safely and adequately swing and leap from tree to tree without crashing on the ground. The oldest and head monkey of the troop decided that Moe and Slick should also learn how to climb mountains safely, so he selected his best climbers and gave them a full-time job of instructing their cousins in the proper way to do mountain climbing.

Back at the plantation, late in the evening, the slave returned with the massive, leather-bound account books for Barclay and Cassiopeia. They decided to wait until the morning to look them over. They wanted to think about things all evening and try to devise an intelligent plan to go forward with freeing their slaves.

Licorice and Black Jack started entertaining the house slaves with their foolish antics. Much laughter was heard from the kitchen, though they tried to suppress the noise that proved an impossibility. They didn't want Master and Mistress to be upset with them for making noise. They were unaware of what Barclay and Cassiopeia thought of slavery. Licorice and Black Jack became instant favorites of the kitchen/house slaves. Smiles were everywhere when the cats were in the room. They lit up every space with joy.

The slaves knew Barclay's uncle as a mean, vicious, money-grubbing owner. He was heartless and would sell any one of them if the price was right. He demanded immediate service and complete obedience. He hated any little offspring of the slaves, and the moment one was born, he found a seller for it. He didn't make much from the sales, but he hated the squirming little animals and the squalling noises they made.

He figured the time they took for their care took time away from what he wanted his servants to do. He was an unloved, frightening slave owner, and none of the servants mourned his passing. They had a fear that the new owner would be worse, but they could do nothing but wait and see what happened when the new master officially took over ownership of the plantation.

The following day, after much turning and tossing, the Barclay's awoke. The plan was to peruse the history of the plantation by scanning all the books. They had a lovely breakfast and retreated to the uncle's study. It contained a large desk and several leather chairs. The windows were from ceiling to floor affording the room plenty of light with which to see.

It took until evening to make sense of all the information contained in the reams of paperwork. When finally, Barclay and Cassiopeia could figure it out, they decided that the plantation could work even if they freed every one of the slaves. They thought they could make the estate a co-op, with each freeman earning a salary and operating their patch of Earth. The idea was probably the first time this thought flittered through the mind of any slave owner in Africa, but Barclay and Cassiopeia were first-time owners and were entirely opposed to being slave owners.

One of the kitchen slaves knocked timorously on the study door, Barclay bid her enter. She looked so frightened, he did not know what had happened, but he thought it must be an enormous incident for her to look so devastated. When she was able to speak in her broken tongue, she informed him and Cassiopeia that a baby had just been born, and the servant asked him what she must do with it.

Barclay and Cassiopeia looked at her in askance, what on Earth do you want us to do with it? They thought they misunderstood her. Then she told them what usually happened to newborns at the plantation. Barclay and Cassiopeia were stunned; they said to her that the ridding of infants would cease immediately.

From then on, any baby born was to be kept and cared for by its mother. The servant stood there and wept. What a mess, Barclay thought. He asked Cassiopeia to escort her back to the kitchen while he got himself together. Barclay took out his handkerchief and blew his nose, and it sounded like a foghorn. After that, he felt better.

After questioning the servants further, the Barclays discovered that his uncle would trade the babies for children between the ages of 8 and 14. Those he would use to drive wagons with water and provisions to the respective fields for the mid-day meals. These children were also used to cut the grass, mow the extensive lawn, and trim all the plantation's fancy hedges.

What kind of person would commit this horrendous act? He was disgusted and ashamed to be related to such a creature. He wanted to correct all the harmful actions previously perpetrated on all the current slaves. He uttered a prayer for all those who were gone and victimized by his uncle.

Barclay called the overseers to the manor. They came right away, wanting to meet the new owner and make a good impression on him. After all, they had worked for Barclay's uncle for years, and he had no complaints at all. Once the overseers arrived, gathered, and were seated, Barclay and Cassiopeia began to explain the day's new order. The slaves were to be immediately marched down to the ocean to bathe; new clothes were to be issued to them, then they were to be returned to gather on the front lawn to be told what the modern-day was going to bring. The overseers said all the slaves were working in the fields, and it was not easy to corral them on a whim. Barclay said this was not a whim, but his order and any overseer who did not want to follow his rules could collect his pay and leave immediately.

With that, the overseers hustled out to gather the field hands, have them wash, change clothes, and return with them to the house. In a couple of hours, there was a massive gathering of slaves on the front lawn. The murmuring was like a swarm of angry bees. There was a sea of black faces everywhere as far as the eye could see. The smell of fear was palpable. Each slave was frightened of the future. Life had been miserable at best, but fear of the unknown was worse.

Barclay was upset as he could not speak their language and wanted them to understand what he was trying to say. He asked the overseers which one of them could communicate in the primary dialects of the slaves. One man came forward; his name was Santiago. He was initially a trader of animal skins, going from tribe to tribe; this enabled him to learn many African dialects. He had lived among the Africans, both free and slaves, for many years.

Santiago hated being an overseer. However, his family was about to lose their farm, and the money from this job was more than he could earn anywhere else. All the slaves under his control respected him, as he was fair and treated them all with as much dignity and respect as was possible.

Barclay got a bullhorn for Santiago; he began to speak and bade Santiago translate for him. He said he didn't care how long it took; he wanted every slave to understand his intent and what future was in store for all of them if they decided to stay on the plantation. The plantation owner began to speak, as Santiago hesitated several times to assure the translation was correct. When he finally decided it was, he explained in most of the African dialects. The slaves could not believe their ears. They bent over with disbelief; they swayed, moaned, and took the information in doubt.

Barclay said subsequently, all the slaves on the plantation, bar none, would be freed. He promised to have papers prepared in the next several days for each of them. Next, Barclay offered to rent a boat to take those to the African mainland, should any of them want to return to their homes. He would also provide all those leaving the region with a small stipend to start a new life of freedom.

He would draw up papers turning his plantation into a co-op for the rest, which meant each ex-slave would own a small share of the residuals. They would earn a salary, eight hours a day for eight hours pay, five days a week they would be expected to work if they were well. If they were sick, they would have Barclay's doctor tend to them. Saturday and Sunday would be free each week to be spent with family, till their gardens, or enjoyed as they would.

Each individual would render an honest day's work; should anyone feel that they did not want to work, they should make arrangements to depart by the next boat. The A ship would leave once a month. Those people going would also be given a small amount of money. This effort must be on the part of everyone. All must work for the greater good, and everyone should contribute as a full member of the co-op.

Each co-op member got a small plot of land to till fresh vegetables for their consumption. They would once again be free to pray to the God of their choice.

There would be new construction of all the current huts in which the slaves lived. New buildings were built by the ex-slaves, which had adequate light, an entrance and exit door, and several separate rooms to provide privacy to the dwellers. As that happened, the builders destroyed the present huts. He realized it would take some time to understand all of this, but patience was the keyword.

He also planned to hire several English teachers to tutor every slave to read and write the English language. Education, he thought, was the key to power and the ability to provide and sustain oneself. The slaves were overwhelmed, and tears poured from most of their eyes.

By this time, all the overseers were struck dumb. They were told they could keep their jobs but only as supervisors. Salaries would remain the same, but there would be no more beatings, the degrading and humiliation of all peoples would cease. If they did not like these terms, they were free to depart with their severance pay on the boat that Barclay hired to take the slaves who wanted to go back to the mainland.

Santiago became head supervisor, and subsequently, was expected to communicate with any and every ex-slave and make their concerns heard. The promotion gave Santiago a generous increase in salary, and he was grateful to have it. He could bring his family to Columbar and provide living quarters for them.

After the long dissertation, Barclay was exhausted, as was Cassiopeia. There was much grumbling from the overseers, but they could do nothing about these new events. The house slaves came from inside the house to stare and listen to these glad tidings. They, too, could not believe their eyes or ears. They all realized they must decide, return home or stay in Columbar as co-op owners with Mr. and Mrs. Barclay.

By this time, Licorice and Black Jack were out on the porch and realized something unusual must be happening. When they saw the chains falling to the ground, they knew, for sure, it was! They leaped in the air, cavorted, rolled over, and ran hither and thither. Everyone was delighted with their joyful antics.

Mr. Barclay asked Cassiopeia if she would take charge of the kitchen. He wanted her to instruct, as best she could, the cooks to slaughter several lambs and cattle to feed the hungry slaves. She immediately took to it like a duck to water. The kitchen help loved her on the spot, and she explained what Mr. Barclay wanted. They went to the gardens and culled vegetables returning with baskets full. They had several slaves dig a massive trench on the lower portion of the lawn, slaughtered the livestock, and began a meat roast to end all meat roasts. Of course, Licorice and Black Jack were watched closely for fear they steal some meat off the roasting pit. Those greedy little devils were not to be trusted!

When called, the slaves timidly approached the pits with the roasting meat. Never in their captivity had they been treated to a meal such as this, no pork, just lamb and beef, within their dietary restrictions. The fresh vegetables were heaped on tables a mile long and a mile high, or so it appeared. They were permitted to walk up, take tin pans, and be served by of all people, the house slaves.

Never! Never! Never! My Lord, what a treat this was. Having been starved for such a long time, many had belly aches and stomach troubles after eating their fill. Barclay told Santiago to explain they must eat slowly for their digestive systems to become once again accustomed to eating correctly. He promised they would always have food while living on Columbar Island. The cats ate like there was no tomorrow, but what did one expect of such gluttonous little creatures?

The following day Mr. Barclay sent for Mr. Tweed. The barrister had no idea for what, but he hurried to the plantation. It wouldn't do to rile the new owners up so that they would fire him. He had been the attorney for Mr. Barclay's uncle for years, and his pocket stayed fat from doing that job. He did not want to change that one bit.

When he arrived, he noticed a subtle change in things. None of the slaves in the yard were wearing chains! He did not think that prudent. He was going to share that information with Barclay pronto. After riding up to the door, he entered. He went into the study. He sat down and awaited the Barclays. They arrived in short order and asked him if he wished for some refreshment.

Being the hoggish fellow he was, he accepted. They rang the bell, and when the young lady appeared, they asked her for some tea and sweet cakes with a smile. She dashed out to fulfill the request. In no time, she returned with a tray laden with sweet cream-filled scones and butter topped raspberry jam cakes and black tea, which she placed on the table.

Mr. Barclay and Cassiopeia wanted to get down to facts right away.

They told Mr. Tweed of the past evening's events. He was aghast. It looked as though the barrister was going to have a heart attack. His face turned purple, eyes bulged, and he started gasping and had to loosen his bow tie to get air.

Sputtering, the barrister coughed and gagged. He fell backward in his chair and turned over the plate of sweet cakes; they dropped to the floor and scattered everywhere on the beautiful Persian carpet. Finally, after drinking some water, he composed himself. "Never has such craziness been heard. It is just not done. What are you two thinking? Your ideas will disrupt the entire system of Africa. Whoever heard of such a thing? What will the rest of the blacks expect when they hear that you have manumitted all of your slaves? They will not only want the same thing but will try to demand it. We'll have an insurrection on our hands. We will not be able to control the animals; there are more of them here than us! No, no, not only no, but absolutely NO."

Mr. Barclay and Cassiopeia sat calmly nibbling on cream-filled scones and sugar-coated jellied cakes while sipping tea from beautiful china cups. Mr. Tweed's tirade did not bother them one bit. The plantation was theirs, and they planned to handle their affairs as they saw fit. Never mind how things were, this was how it was going to be in the future! That was their final say, and if Mr. Tweed wanted to tend his resignation, he was free to do so; they would accept it gladly. If he wanted to stay in their employ, he would immediately begin drafting up manumission papers for each slave on the premises. That was his final order.

Mr. Barclay ended the conversation. Licorice and Black Jack were watching Mr. Tweed gleefully and hoping some more cakes would make the carpet, and they could once again clean them up any mess the sloppy fellow made. Oh, happy day, one man's catastrophe is another cat's pleasure!

Mr. Tweed's new task was to recruit and hire teachers to educate the residents of Columbar. He rolled his eyes in exasperation with the thought of teaching low animals, but he had no choice but to comply with the order.

Finally, after much hemming and hawing, sputtering, and coughing, Mr. Tweed said he wanted to keep his job so he would draw up the papers starting that afternoon. He was, of course, fearful what the other slave owners would say or do when they found out about this plan. He staggered off to his horse with a mess of cream and jelly crumbs down his waistcoat and rode down the walk forlorn, dreading having to face the other plantation owners eventually when they became aware of these events.

After Barclay's conversation with Mr. Tweed, he realized there might be a significant danger for all of them once the other owners realized he had freed the slaves. He called for the blacksmith and requested he melt all the shackles, make a mold for musket balls, and pour the dissolved iron into the casts to fabricate as many musket balls as possible.

Barclay and Cassiopeia drove their carriage to town later that day. They spoke to a ship's Captain who had recently docked and was searching for a buyer of firearms. Luckily, he and Barclay came to an immediate agreement to buy five-hundred new muskets and several wagon loads of musket balls. Barclay contracted for several dock hands to load the wagons and drive them back to his estate.

Licorice and Black Jack rode along for company as they wanted to see the sailors on the Fair Winds. When the wagon stopped, they hopped off and boarded the vessel. They greeted their shipmates. Everyone was ecstatic to see the brother cats. Captain Schiff was still out of town arranging for the purchase of gems.

The cats stayed for a little while as they needed to remain with Barclay and Cassiopeia until the Captain came for them. They were also looking forward to meeting Moe and Slick's extended family when they came to visit. So, they hopped up on the wagon and rode back with Barclay and Cassiopeia. The carts with the muskets and balls followed behind.

Upon arrival, everyone unloaded the carts and the muskets and balls were placed in a locked storehouse. Barclay decided all hands who wanted to live on Columbar Island needed to learn how to shoot a rifle. Their freedom now won must be defended at all costs.

First, the overseers came one by one to inform Barclay of their decision to stay or go. Four said they were leaving. They were utterly opposed to black "animals," as they called the ex-slaves roaming free. The two remaining, Santiago and one other, would be kept very busy at first, trying to supervise such a large crew of remaining workers.

Four hundred fifty of the freedmen opted to stay on the island. The other fifty were grateful for their freedom but had families elsewhere, and they wanted desperately to locate and rejoin them. Despite their limited ability to communicate, they thanked Barclay and Cassiopeia for their freedom and promised they would do anything for them anytime needed.

Barclay commissioned a ship and told the Captain he would need his services monthly. The Captain was happy to oblige and promised to sail from the mainland to Columbar regularly to pick up passengers and provisions and drop any stores the island residents required.

Barclay gave each of the departing individuals a small bag of gold to get started in a new life and watched them sail away with their manumission papers tightly grasped in their hands. He prayed they would have happy, successful lives in the future. He was miserable about past events, where his uncle proved to be such an evil man, and how many lives he had ruined and adversely affected.

None of the house slaves wanted to leave. They, too, were happy to have their freedom and to be paid for their labor. Never, in their wildest imaginings did they envision such an event happening to them. They adored Barclay and Cassiopeia and worked like Trojans to please them.

Licorice and Black Jack, of course, became star attractions for everyone. They were everywhere, in everything, on everything with their playful antics. Meanwhile, the entire monkey troop sneaked aboard a covered wagon to come to the plantation undetected. The wagon driver wondered why the horses were plodding at such a slow pace, and no manner of urging them could convince them to drive faster. He didn't know that the old horses carried the additional load of sixty-five little lemurs and his original cargo.

Finally, the wagon with the monkeys came up to the Barclay plantation, and the broad canvas cover ripped off and out scampered Moe, Slick, and their entire family of the monkeys. What a wonderful surprise! Licorice and Black Jack were delighted to see their friends and meet the monkey troop. Barclay and Cassiopeia laughed until their sides ached with all the monkeyshines. They paid the driver a handful of silver for delivering the little monkeys safely.

The following day the ex-slaves were called to the mansion and told they would learn to shoot the firearms Barclay had acquired. Santiago translated for Barclay, and he said he hoped they would never need to use them, but better for them to be safe than sorry. They all agreed, and after being put on schedules, between working the fields, each one took turns learning to fire the muskets.

Meanwhile, the townspeople of Columbar were up in arms. Just as Mr. Tweed predicted, the word of the mass freeing caught fire. There were many people grumbling and complaining about this unheard-of event. Most of the slaves who knew it demanded their immediate freedom. First, not many of the slave owners were as wealthy as Mr. and Mrs. Barclay. They did not have the unlimited funds to pay and educate their chattel. They only thought of the blacks as their property that they spent good gold for and who had no intention of setting free for any reason. They intended for them to produce other slaves and work until they died. That was the expected future of all slaves, and rightly so!

Further, they could not read or write, for if they could, they might get the insane impression they were as good as or better than their owners. Many of the owners could not read either and did not want their property to do so. The slave owners had many ugly thoughts about their "property." They were afraid of them in actuality, for they outnumbered their white owners one hundred to one.

They had a great fear of the slaves for their customs were unknown, and most people, instead of seeking knowledge of the unfamiliar, find it easier to dismiss it with hate and bigotry. Beating and demeaning their property was a way to keep them in fearful submission.

One evening a meeting was held in the town hall. Someone brought a cask of rum, which fired up those in attendance. After drinking, cursing, and rabblerousing, they decided to storm Barclay's mansion. The idea was to kill as many slaves as possible and put things right. They would burn the estate down to the ground and run both of the Barclays out of town. Those slaves left could be divided among themselves as an incentive for joining their "righteous army!"

The ex-slaves quickly grasped handling the muskets, and they patrolled the perimeter day and night. They rotated their assigned tasks. Being assigned this duty made them very happy. Everyone wanted to keep their conclave safe. Moe and Slick, along with their family troop, watched the proceedings and decided to maintain watch with them.

What a sight, men with muskets over their shoulders and monkeys running back and forth, chattering away to each other. If it weren't because the situation was so dire, it would be comical. The monkeys never seemed to tire. They performed watch most of the day and night; their energy was boundless. At the same time, the guards had to rotate their watches to get some rest.

If someone arrived with ill-intent, he would never suspect a troop of monkeys acting as guards. Life went along pleasantly for a while. Captain Schiff returned from his mine trip; he was about ready to sail for Amsterdam. He stopped by the Barclay's to pick up Licorice and Black Jack. Mr. and Mrs. Barclay invited him to stay the night.

They said he would be able to leave at daybreak and get a rest; they wanted to hear all about his trip and see the gemstones he had acquired. The Captain felt honored by their invitation and decided to accept it. Being exhausted from his travels, he welcomed the thought of a soft bed, if only for one night.

Captain Schiff showed the Barclay's his bag of gems, and they were astounded. The stones were the size of pigeon's eyes; whatever they were placed in would be beautiful beyond description. He put the gems back in his knapsack with a feeling of accomplishment. Soon the journey would be over, and he could get some much-needed rest, to say nothing of seeing his lovely Lady Veronica.

Barclay and Cassiopeia told Captain Schiff about their decision to free their slaves and turn their plantation into a profit-sharing co-op; the Captain was amazed. He thought it a fantastic idea, but he, like Mr. Tweed, knew this would be a dangerous and challenging endeavor. Anyone attempting to change a system so lucrative for so many years would find it almost impossible.

This news would stir up events so that they would have to be cautious of their every move. None of the other slave owners shared their views and only wished to maintain the status quo, to live their lazy, indulgent lives, and continue their luxurious way of life with little physical effort on their part.

They talked long into the night; Licorice and Black Jack huddled under the Captain's chair. They were so happy to see him and knew they were about to leave for another sea voyage aboard the Fair Winds. They enjoyed their visit to the mansion, and spending time with Moe and Slick was great, but it was now the moment for their departure. They wanted to live what they considered their routine lives only when they were at sea.

This land thing was O.K., but it was nothing like their existence on the listing, rolling deck of their glorious ship. They could look around for miles while climbing the lanyards and scanning the sea from the crow's nest. That was the life! They nodded off quickly because they knew the Captain never dropped any crumbs on the floor while he ate, so there was no fear of them missing a tidbit or two, more's the pity.

Captain Schiff was provided a sumptuous meal and shown to a beautiful bedroom on the second floor. He was amazed at the luxurious appointments. He quickly dropped off to sleep. In the middle of the night, there were noises, and the entire house awoke. The house servants were knocking on everyone's doors to stir the folks within. When Barclay and Captain Schiff roused themselves, they realized that there was trouble outside.

Santiago and the other overseer had opened the arms storehouse and began distributing muskets with musket balls to each ex-slave. They were eager to get the firearms because this was about their remaining free or losing their lives. They had felt a taste of what freedom felt like and was not willing to give it up in any way. They knew they would rather die than become slaves ever again. The decision, among them, was to fight to the death if needed.

The monkeys were howling and chattering loudly. Licorice and Black Jack jumped up and rushed out the front door. They saw shadowy people at a distance in the front yard.

The cats ran into the people and started biting and scratching at the ragged band of individuals who headed the assailants' front line. The monkeys joined the fray. The mismatch brigand of folks was startled to be attacked by monkeys and cats, of all things. The confusion gave

Santiago and his fellow supervisor time to distribute the muskets to every ex-slave in the vicinity.

Barclay told the female servants and Cassiopeia to remain indoors. He and Captain Schiff ran out and got guns and ammunition. They loaded their firearms and began shooting into the shadows. Some of them fell instantly. Attempting to enter the Barclay estate, the crowd had no right arms to do so successfully. They had to fall back and scatter almost as soon as they started their raid. Off they were routed quickly, and the rest of the evening remained uneventful. Everyone tried sleeping, though they only got partial rest, for they had to be ever vigilant of another attack.

The townspeople realized that the Barclays conclave was well-equipped to protect them. They knew they had better make a sounder plan if they were to overcome the island's inhabitants. Meanwhile, Captain Schiff departed with Licorice and Black Jack.

Unfortunately, he could not linger any longer, for his commission was to deliver the gems as soon as possible, and several events had already delayed him in his quest. Upon arrival in town, he discovered the inhabitants were all in an uproar. They were running helter-skelter, with no plan other than pulling the wounded people from their wagons and attempting to help those shot during the previous night's raid.

They held a meeting again, and this was an unheard-of circumstance, they said and weren't sure what they could do about it or how to solve it. Finally, the townspeople decided to purchase firearms from any incoming ship that had some for sale. The Barclay's had exhausted all available supplies. The Captain dispatched a sailor back to the

Barclay's to inform them of the townspeople's plan, thereby alerting them to the impending danger.

Licorice and Black Jack never solved their quandary about being black. They knew wherever the cats traveled; being beautiful, people admired them. Most people wanted to own them, and many had tried capturing the duo.

Questions remain why blacks continue being reviled and mistreated still exist. Maybe someday, they thought, people will learn to love each other equally and realize all are brothers in every way.

With a heavy heart, Captain Schiff lifted anchor and set sail for Amsterdam with Licorice and Black Jack. He did not want to leave the Barclay commune, but he had his commission and could not ignore that. He did pray for their good fortune and wished them well. The Captain planned one day to return to Columbar Island to see how they had fared.

The Barclay's, now forewarned, were vigilant in their knowledge that the slave owners and town bullies might return to attack them any time. It was not until approximately six months later that they tried several times more to overpower the estate. By then, the members of the entire commune had become highly proficient in the use of firearms. The marksmen put down the insurrections within several hours.

None of the inhabitants were ever severely hurt. They just obtained a few minor scratches; the attackers, however, suffered severe losses over several tries of wasting numerous hours attempting to overcome the conclave. They ultimately realized that attacking the Barclay estate was futile. The residents were too well supplied with arms and exceedingly proficient in the use of them.

In their travels, several ships' captains had heard of their plight and made special trips to dock at Columbar Island to provide the Barclay's with additional firearms and anything they needed to sustain their position of maintaining freedom for their residents. They also transported teachers, several nurses, and two more doctors to the island. The people learned to speak, read and write English, and ultimately converse with each other. There was very little discontent on the island, as all were grateful for their status and never wanted it to change.

Peace reigned on Columbar Island; the monkey troop visited regularly and performed many carousing antics for everyone. After the band observed how Moe and Slick acted with Cassiopeia and Barclay, they gradually learned to trust the man-creatures and would allow people to pet them. One afternoon, a youngster came running to the house. He knocked frantically on the kitchen door.

The cook opened it and asked him what she could do for him. He said one of the monkeys was playing with a giant red stone in the yard, and it didn't look like any rock he had ever seen. The cook came out and saw the monkey, she thought, this was not just any stone, but possibly a ruby! The servant tried wresting the jewel from the monkey, but he wasn't having any of it. She returned to the house and went to see Cassiopeia.

When she told Cassiopeia the story, Mrs. Barclay went outside to see for herself. Sure enough, there was the monkey with a massive stone in its paw. Since the ape wasn't going to give it up without a fight, she told several youngsters to watch it and see where it went. She was sure she could find it.

The children mowed the lawn and did their yard duties, all the while watching the little lemur. After a time, it loped off to the woods with them closely behind. After a long trek, they followed the ape to a cave hidden deep in a mountainside. Once the monkey entered the cave, they also did. There were gemstones everywhere; what a find, it was a ruby mine of great value.

They rushed off to tell Mr. and Mrs. Barclay of their find. Once the Barclay's were aware of it, they were delighted. They knew from that time on the tiny island would be a self-sufficient co-op and provide for each member of their group. They never would they have to worry about losing what they had earned.

Columbar Island was considered free for all ex-slaves. It was left alone by all other slave owners. The freemen found great happiness being able to live their lives without fear every day. Barclay, Cassiopeia, Moe, and Slick were superbly content to live at peace in an environment of love and harmony.

Licorice, Black Jack, and Pepper the Parrot

After departing Columbar Island, the Fair Winds set sail for Amsterdam. Licorice and Black Jack were once again sailing on that beautiful vessel. What a glorious feeling, they thought. Sailing is the life for us and the only way we can be completely safe and happy. Every time we make the mistake of going ashore, we get in a heap of trouble. It is best to be here on the ship's deck, where everyone loves and cares for us, they thought. There will be no more crazy, forgetful witches, no mad furriers, no bloodthirsty butchers or greedy rat catchers. There would be only fantastic free-thinking sailors and the glorious blue sea, fluffy clouds and white sails, seagulls, whales, and dolphins to see and enjoy—what an excellent thought.

The ship had loaded her supplies, and it carried a full complement of able hands. No scoundrels, no rapscallions, no more shiftless sailors like Klutz Hare Brain, no thieves, thank goodness. Everyone was in a positive mood. The Fair Winds was home to the cats, but to Captain Schiff, it provided his livelihood. He considered his home in Liverpool, where Veronica and his aged parents lived. He missed them terribly.

The Captain loved sailing and enjoyed that way of life but wanted to return home once in a while. He had been at sea for such a long time; in fact, this trip was the most extended voyage he'd ever made without stopping off to see about the welfare of his friends and relatives.

Captain Schiff was delighted to have Licorice and Black Jack sail with him. He considered them as close as any family member he had, and they made being away so long less miserable for him. They, of course, loved him equally.

The cats got into several dangerous scrapes on the voyage, but they eventually always seemed to get out of them, thank goodness. So, far, the Captain had to pay 1,000 doubloons twice for their return because of their wild shenanigans. Even with that happening, he thought they were worth it, for they had saved the crew a lot of money by keeping the rat population down.

Rampant vermin could destroy much of the cargo when they nibbled on the grain and ran amuck. They would eat the foodstuffs, rip the bags open, and foul everything their filthy tracks ran through and touched. Captain Schiff was grateful for the little feline brother's help.

Besides being the world's best ratters, they were full of joyous pranks and fun-filled escapades. They entertained the crew when things became dull. At times the ship would be becalmed and drift due to no wind to fill the sails, and then the seamen would become impatient and argumentative with each other. When that happened, several fights would break out over the slightest, unimportant incidents. Controlling a crew of bored, restless, lively men proved to be a daunting task for the Captain and his first mate.

After Licorice and Black Jack were born and grew a bit, things changed for the better. They provided laughs for everyone. They had learned, previously on one of their wild jaunts, to read Tarot cards, and they were good at it! Sailors, being a superstitious lot, always wanted their fortunes told. Better yet, it didn't cost anything when the cat brothers did it. Having your future told was costly when it was done by a "so-called psychic," further, most of the time, they were wrong and way off the mark. So, the seamen patiently waited their turn to have the "little fellows" tell them their fortunes.

The cats chased each other up and down the deck and all over the ship. They dashed after rats dispatching them to rat heaven. The brothers bedeviled the Cookie in the mess hall for scraps and treats, sliding up and down the yardarms. Licorice and Black Jack would meow loudly to convince seamen to take them up to the crow's nest. There they would peep out over the vast sea and watch whales and dolphins play for hours. They would nap with their chosen sailor of the night and tell fortunes to those who asked. All these activities kept the little fellows as busy as they could be.

They, of course, were fed choice tidbits whenever the sailors ate. The seaman who gave them the best goody was the one they would select to curl up and sleep through the night. Sometimes they ignored all and slept curled up together in a single black, silken ball. They did that when the ship pitched and tossed in a raging storm.

Other than their tails, the cats were identical. Like all Bombay cats, their coat was shiny black, and their golden eyes were full of naughty fun. The only difference between them was their tails. Licorice's tail was straight and smooth, while Black Jack's had a crinkle in his, thanks to a fleeing rat that knocked over a grappling hook which fell on it! After healing, his tail was never the same, bent forever. That had been Black Jack's pride and joy, and never to be again! He despised rats through and through. Licorice hated them, but not with the intense fervor of hatred his brother had for them!

One night, with no warning, an immense storm suddenly raged with such ferocity that even the most seasoned sailor was frightened. Due to Captain Schiff and his crew's brilliant seamanship, they were able to keep the vessel aright, and they sailed through it with only a ripped sail or two.

The following day they spotted several men adrift hanging on planks of wood which was the remains of the wreck of parts of a ship. There was, of all things, a bedraggled parrot floating on her board. From what they could gather, this was once a pirate ship, as evidenced by the skull and cross bone flag in shreds wrapped around one of the floating masts.

The sailing code of conduct of the open sea dictated no matter who you were or what you had done. A ship must rescue anyone whose vessel was distressed or lost at sea. The crew didn't want to take the motley group of sailors aboard but could not deny them a helping hand due to their miserable circumstances. They threw a rope ladder known as "Jacob's Ladder" down for the sailors to grasp and come aboard. There were four of them. After which, the Fair Winds' crew lassoed the parrot and pulled it up over the side.

The parrot was squawking loudly. "Avast, ye bilge rats; ye need to be keelhauled for treating me this way." Evidently, she didn't like them dragging her about, but there was no other solution; it was either pull her aboard or leave her to drown. The Parrot trade was famous around the world. The trade value of an exotic bird made finding one a prize. The crew kept her for sale at a later date to some wealthy bird collector. The pirate captain was always threatening to sell her at the next port, and she never knew what would happen. She disliked the wicked man intensely.

The rescued sailors said the parrot's name was Pepper, and she once belonged to their deceased Captain. She was hatched in the Congo in Africa and was highly intelligent. She had a vocabulary of approximately two-hundred words and was ever learning more. She could mimic human speech, especially that of her owner. Several times she uttered an order, and they obeyed it, by mistake, thinking it was their Captain speaking.

They imagined since the Fair Winds' crew saved it; she would now be the property of the ship's Captain. Pepper ate fruit, nuts, seeds, insects, and tree bark. She loved pears, oranges, apples, and bananas. They thought she was approximately twenty years old but weren't sure.

Once the bird was on deck, Licorice and Black Jack spotted it. They didn't know what to think. It didn't look like their friends Moe and Slick; they wondered what on earth this thing was. Hard to tell, they thought, it wasn't like any creature they had ever seen.

The beast was gray and white, with red under-tail feathers. It had large gray speckled rounded feet, the color of Pepper, the spice. She had two toes in front and two in the back on which she could perch on limbs and the ship's rails. Her beak was huge; it was curved and jet black. Not only that, but she could also talk and converse with the Captain and crew. The cats couldn't figure it out. It was not a human, not a monkey, not a dog. What could it be? It hobbled up to them after a while and said, "hi, my name is Pepper, what's yours?"

They, of course, couldn't answer her, but the Captain told the bird their names are Licorice and Black Jack. With her wings clipped, she tottered around the deck. The bird chattered from dawn to dusk about her adventures on the pirate ship to anyone who would listen. Finally, Licorice and Black Jack decided they liked the parrot, and she, in turn, was immediately fond of them. Several times she hopped up on one or the other cat's back and rode around shouting, "heave-ho me hearties." Making the crew laugh and want to see the trick over and over again.

After learning what Pepper ate, Captain Schiff made sure she had the best. He liked the little bird and enjoyed her tales of piracy. He also was glad she entertained the crew, for a happy team made for smooth sailing. The bird appeared to be content to be owned by the Captain, and she liked Licorice, Black Jack, and the seamen of the Fair Winds. The Captain had no intention of selling or giving her away. Like Licorice and Black Jack, she had become a permanent member of his entourage.

At night Captain Schiff placed Pepper in his cabin to sleep at all other times she was parading around the deck entertaining one and all. She was a raucous old bird and could sing pirates ditties by the dozen and tell the sailors rowdy stories of pirate life. The seamen never tired of hearing them. She repeatedly screamed for a tankard of grog, which made the crew double up with laughter.

Pepper mightily entertained them. The bird proved valuable to Licorice and Black Jack, too, by spotting sly rats and screaming at the top of her voice, "RATS, give them no quarter!" The cats got the message quickly and caught several of the sneaky devils they might have missed at first had Pepper not spotted them and sounded the alarm.

The pirates were a nasty bunch and did not mingle with the crew in any way. They ate everything in sight and were not even appreciative of being saved from drowning or eaten by hungry sharks. Never did one of the four rescued rascals say thank you. They never volunteered to assist in any of the ship's duties. They just wanted to loll around, play the fife and fiddle, dance jigs, drink grog, and be fed. The pirates were only waiting for the next port to depart and find another brigantine to join!

The Fair Winds crew grumbled among themselves about having to do all the work while the pirates did nothing, but Captain Schiff said they had done a good deed, and there was no need to complain about it. He assured his men they would rid themselves of their unpleasant company as soon as they spotted the next available seaport or a proper landing place to cast them ashore. The sailors of the Fair Winds didn't trust their unsavory guests and watched them like hawks.

At first, the pirates teased and tormented Licorice and Black Jack, but the crew made short shrift of that and told the unwashed, ragged bunch of brigands the cats were members of their team mistreatment was not tolerated. The next one who dared to hurt or even thought of harming the cats would be given the "old heave-ho," off the side of the Fair Winds, back to Davey Jones' Locker, from where they came.

The crew would provide no planks or anything to hold on to, so those who couldn't swim would be out of luck. Anyone in the waters would need to swim faster than the sharks, which was highly unlikely. They were sure the hungry school of sharks would be glad to retrieve their lost meal of four tasty buckos.

From that moment on, Licorice and Black Jack were no longer tormented and were given a wide berth by the loathsome pirates. Most bandits are bullies. They are great for performing foul deeds when they are in a group, but they do not prove brave once alone. The pirates never bothered Pepper, for she would bite and scratch them. Her beak was huge; once the bird bit them, they would not soon forget.

Several of the pirates had scars on their fingers and arms from previous occurrences. The spots were evidence that she would not tolerate anyone trying to pester or torment her. Once they had experienced that, they never attempted it again.

Pepper watched Licorice, and Black Jack read Tarot for the members of the crew. In a short time, she could do it too. Not only could the bird read the cards, but Pepper could tell the sailors, in a word, their meaning. She was a wonder! Between the parrot, Licorice, and Black Jack, the sailors hastened to finish their daily chores so they could enjoy the entertainment provided by the trio of intelligent animals. Pepper's droppings made a mess all over the ship; they were evidence of anywhere she went. Mopping the deck several times as needed, the seamen thought she paid for the extra trouble by telling "tall tales," Tarot reading, and singing new jingles for them.

The crew decided to hold a surprise birthday party for Captain Schiff. The evening of the event, the Captain retired to his cabin, taking Pepper with him. Once he was in his quarters, the Cookie took out a cake from the brick oven he had baked and put tin plates and tankards on the mess hall table. The first mate broke out a cask of rum, and everyone prepared to have a spectacular celebration.

They sent the cabin boy to fetch the Captain, and upon arrival, after seeing all the preparations, he was pleasantly surprised. Meanwhile, unnoticed, one of the pirates snuck into the Captain's cabin and searched for something of value to steal. He didn't realize Pepper was there watching him because the Captain, when called by the crew, left and forgot to cover her cage.

The pirate found a large box stored under the Captain's bunk. He pulled it out and began rifling through it. He was amazed at what he discovered. It held the fortune of sapphires and rubies meant for delivery to the Master Jeweler in Amsterdam. The parrot watched the pirate through half-closed eyes. Just as he withdrew his hand, crammed full of precious stones, Pepper shouted, "Ahoy, Matey, man's in the box." With that, the Captain and crew rushed to the cabin and caught the thief "red-handed."

They tied the culprit up and placed him in confinement in the bilge's brig. Afterward, the crew continued to enjoy their Captain's birthday celebration. The thief's companions were sulky and demanded more than their share of the rum. "No more drink," said the Captain, as a drunken crew could be a dangerous crew.

Every member needed to be alert and capable of handling the ship at all times, and being intoxicated would not be the right situation to find oneself in. Even though the seamen received no help from the pirates, the Captain didn't want them stumbling around, passed out, or in the way, in case an emergency arose.

Several days later, the Fair Winds neared the shore of a tiny, sandy island. Captain Schiff ordered the four pirates to disembark. He provided them with a bit of water and provisions. At first, the pirates refused to go because the island looked uninhabited, possibly marooning them. The Captain said, "you have no choice, you either take the boat with the provisions, or we will dump you in the drink where we found you, with nothing but the rags on your ungrateful backs. What's your pleasure?" He asked.

Of course, they decided to take the stores and little boat, hoping that another ship might pass by and rescue them. They were furious with their shipmate for being so stupid to get caught stealing from the Fair Winds, thus making them leave. They wanted to be put ashore at a large port city because the chance of finding another pirate ship was higher than being deserted on some lonely island, but it was too late for regrets.

As soon as the Captain saw the pirates pull their boat ashore, he ordered the Fair Winds to weigh the anchor and set sail for their proper course. That done, all the crew were relieved to have the pirates gone forever. They hoped they would never have to pick up any more thieves or brigands again.

The Fair Winds sailed on, and all the crew set out to happily do their duties with no quarrel or argument whatever. Licorice, Black Jack, and Pepper told fortunes and played games aboard the ship with abandon. They were no longer worried about any more scurrilous knaves, and life was great for them again.

Pepper, however, kept telling "tall tales" about buried treasure. No one paid her much attention, for she was ever spouting off about imaginary happenings, so they just let her prattle. The bird provided entertainment on an otherwise dull trip every day. There was always something new she had to say or a new song she could sing for them.

One evening when the Captain and Pepper were alone in his cabin, she recited the tale again. This time Captain Schiff listened intently to her entire story. Pepper spoke of an island near the coast of Columbar where her pirate crew had stashed many chests of gold, silver, and jewels. She said, when pirates captured people from any ship, they would make prisoners of them. Once they came ashore, they forced their hostages to accompany them where the treasures were. There they were forced to dig large pits in which to bury the swag. After planting the jewels, the crew left the hostages on the island. They had no provisions. Thus, they died of starvation or thirst or at the very least went mad and killed each other. The thought being, "dead men tell no tales."

The pirates thought the location of their treasure was safe forever. They didn't take reckon of the fact that Pepper rode the shoulders of the buccaneer each trip he made, knew and remembered the exact location of both the island and the booty. Since the ship Pepper was on sank, it was probable that no one other than she knew its exact location. The pirate didn't trust his deckhands, so he took no one with him other than his prisoners and first mate. He, like the Captain, was dead and gone. The buried treasure's secret might have gone to a watery grave had it not been for Pepper and her remarkable memory.

Captain Schiff unrolled his sheepskin map and scanned it for this island of which Pepper spoke. He found a little spot just 100 nautical miles south of Columbar Island. What to do? He pondered this over and over. He and his crew were anxious to return home after such a long, arduous voyage.

They would make money from the journey and get a share of the profits from the jewels delivered in Amsterdam, but nothing like they would glean if the story were true. He didn't want a disgruntled sailor group if this story was just some fantasy of a talkative bird with a wild imagination. He wanted to wed Veronica. Having a decent amount of money would probably make her parents more amenable to the marriage than the prospect of having seafaring penniless son-in-law.

If the treasure were real, it would assure his ability to support Veronica adequately, and they would want for very little. He also was aware that he had on board adequate provisions to feed the crew if they agreed to change course to visit the place of which the bird spoke.

Finally, after much thought and mulling over, the Captain called all hands on deck and repeated Pepper's story. There was much moaning and groaning from the men. They had all had heard of buried treasures during most of the voyages they took. They only proved to be a drunken sailor's dream or some cruel hoax to get an unsuspecting landlubber to buy a bogus map.

However, several said: "in for a penny, in for a pound. We're out here now. Let's take a chance. Who knows? We might luck out." The thought of such untold riches was too much for them to ignore and possibly pass up. The crew knew they could sail for years and only eke out a meager living, or they might find a "treasure," such as the bird spoke of, and they could live comfortably for the rest of their lives.

Unlike many ship's captains, Captain Schiff was fair and shared all monies earned from every voyage with his crew. Everyone aboard respected him and knew he wasn't taking this story lightly. They also were aware he wanted to go home as desperately as they did, probably even more so. They voted, and all hands decided to prolong their trip and take a chance on finding out if the cache of buried booty was a reality!

He ordered the ship to come about and change course. The Fair Winds headed back in the direction of Columbar Island for the unknown location, and the Captain and members of the crew hoped for the best. They sailed for several days, the lack of winds retarded their progress, but eventually, they sighted the tiny island. They had to use small boats to land there, for jagged rocks surrounded it, and it would have scuttled the ship if she came any closer to it than two miles.

Captain Schiff had the men draw straws to determine who would accompany him and Pepper to look for the treasure. Everyone agreed that was the just way to do it. After the selection, they gathered digging tools and placed them in their boats.

After lowering the Fair Winds' boats, the Captain, Pepper, and thirty men, ten in each boat, rowed to the island. They had to beach the boats securely so they wouldn't drift off. After getting off the boats, the crew walked with great care, taking one step at a time because of the sharp rocks and many jagged seashells that could severely cut their feet to shreds.

The seamen did not have adequate foot cover to protect them from such rugged terrain. Pepper rode on Captain Schiff's shoulders while squawking and flapping her wings furiously. Captain Schiff was sure there must be something to her tale because of her wild enthusiasm.

Once they all gathered on the shore, Pepper jumped down from Captain Schiff's shoulder. She wobbled off in the sand for quite a distance. The crew followed her every step. They found a mountain of bleached bones of human skeletons scattered all over the ground. Cape vultures were flying around in search of food. They had picked the bones clean of these unfortunate folk once they died.

When they saw the men from the boats, they probably thought they would have a banquet. They circled but did not land, for vultures don't attack the living; they only wait for one to be close to death or dead before visiting a body for a meal. After looking at all the deceased's bones, the Captain uttered a silent prayer for them and thought, what a tragedy.

Pepper stopped, plopped down, and screeched, "Dig here, dig here." The men started excavating where the bird indicated after several feet of digging; they heard metallic clinks. They dug deeper, rapidly, and excitedly finding five chests in the ditch. They opened them after hauling them up. The crew discovered unbelievable wealth contained within each coffer. Everyone gasped and could not believe their eyes.

The Captain ordered them to wrap ropes around them and pull the boxes to the shore, which they did. They had to chop down several saplings to make platforms for rolling the caskets over the rocks and shells to the little ships. They could not transport everything at once, so they had to make several trips to retrieve all the boxes. The Captain said, in respect for the dead, they must bury the skeletons properly.

Each sailor took turns covering the bones, praying for the deceased, and finally, the crew left the small island. The sailors filled the boats. Rowing them back to the Fair Winds was a chore but a happy one no seaman minded. The vultures circled sadly, realizing there was no meal to be had for them this time.

After the seamen boarded the Fair Winds, they opened the boxes and showed the booty to the crew's rest. Then they uncorked a cask of rum drinking in celebration of their grand discovery. All had a drink and toasted Pepper for her leading them to the treasure. They even let her dip her beak several times in a tankard as a reward. She used to drink with the pirate crew, but Captain Schiff was not going to tolerate that. He didn't want Pepper to get ill, as he did not know about curing sick birds.

So, a sip would have to suffice. It is better than nothing, she thought; it's been a long dry spell. Licorice and Black Jack were thrilled that the entire crew was so happy, they didn't know the reason, but they knew there were more laughter and revelry than there had been in several months.

The ship was finally headed to Amsterdam to drop off the jewels they had previously collected for the Master

Jeweler, after which they were going to Liverpool, their home port. Everyone was in a state of ecstasy, for they finally were on their way home. It had been so long that they'd been sailing from port to port. On this voyage, they earned more money than they had ever seen in all their travels at sea combined. Believing Pepper's story about the treasure was an intelligent move on everyone's part.

If they would frugally manage their finances, they could pick and choose what voyages they wanted to take, if any. They could even open businesses if they desired and remain ashore with their families. No more begging for a berth on a ship. No more sailing with a captain who was cruel or had a bad reputation. No more being short-changed after a trip when arriving at their port. No more inadequate rest or sleep. No more having no money to buy clothing or food. No more light meals like hardtack or sour beer. They would, at last, be able to provide for their families handsomely. This blessing was what they had all been dreaming of their entire lives. Finding the treasure would improve all of their existence, and it was all due to Pepper's knowledge of the island and the Captain's faith in the parrot. They sailed for several months and finally arrived at their destination.

After landing in Amsterdam's harbor, they dropped off the jewels they brought for the Master Jeweler. He was delighted with the stones and handsomely paid for them. The jeweler thanked Captain Schiff and gave him a bonus for his trouble. Never, he said, had he seen such glorious gems. The goldsmith imagined he could design many exquisite one-of-a-kind pieces for the Royal Family from them. He thought this would make him famous. All the royal members of the realm would want to purchase his wares, securing his livelihood forever, and he and his family could live in comfort.

Next, Captain Schiff located a reputable dealer of treasures and had the items appraised, then converted into cash. He saved several gems for a bracelet for Veronica. As was customary, the purser divided the money. The Captain received one-half of the funds, and the crew split the remaining money equally. Each seaman thanked Captain Schiff profusely.

Most of them stayed on the vessel, while several departed for shore leave and did not report when the ship raised her sails and anchor. Licorice and Black Jack remained aboard the Fair Winds, never leaving the deck. The cats were not going to take a chance of being abandoned or getting into any more trouble losing their opportunity to return home. They wanted to stay with Captain Schiff and Pepper. No more fooling around for them, they thought. The Fair Winds weighed anchor and departed for their home port of Liverpool.

Arriving home, Captain Schiff ordered the anchor dropped. All hands roared with relief and gratitude. They had all missed being with their families. Each crew member gave thanks for their safe return and the prosperous voyage as they hastened off the ship to go home. Captain Schiff would see his lady love, Veronica, and he planned to propose to her at long last.

He took Pepper, Licorice, and Black Jack with him to his parent's home. They were thrilled to see their son. His father was ailing, so the Captain was even happier that he arrived when he did. His family was in the throes of losing their home, for his father could no longer work due to his illness, and they had no money left. They told him their news but said Veronica had visited daily, bringing food she cooked for them. The Captain was happy about her kindness and couldn't wait to see her.

Both the Captain's father and mother liked the cats, as they had owned several in the past but were a little wary about the bird. Once they heard her talk, they grew a little fonder of her. However, they were not fond of the mess she made as she walked all over the house. Then Captain Schiff told them about the treasure, and they decided they could quickly love the parrot. She had saved them from the almshouse for sure.

Knocking was heard at the front door; the bailiff presented the Captain's parents with a "vacate the premises" note. It said they had one week to remove their personal belongings and get out. The Captain laughed and asked him where he should pay the rent that was in arrears. The bailiff wondered why he appeared amused after receiving such dire news, but he told him in any case. Captain Schiff hastened to the rental office and paid all the back rent. Their son then went to an office that sold real estate and selected a small cottage with a garden in the suburbs for his parents and paid in full for the property.

He returned to his parent's home with the key and deed in hand and presented both the property papers and the door key to them. They were speechless. He told them that he would hire a cart and several draymen to move all of their possessions to their new home the next day. Meanwhile, he wanted to pay a visit to Veronica and her parents.

He washed and put on his formal uniform. He scooped up Pepper, Licorice, and Black Jack; he figured they were his family. He didn't plan to marry anyone who could not accept living with his pets. He took the sapphire necklace he intended to give Veronica as an engagement gift if she and her father agreed to his proposal and gave consent to the marriage.

Upon arrival at Veronica's parent's house, he knocked at the door. She opened it and discovered it was him; she immediately fell into his arms. Pepper screeched loudly, and the cats became squished with all the hugging and kissing. They couldn't even get into the house. What a noisy, crazy time that was!

After settling down, she bid him enter. She showed him into their parlor and called her mother and father. They came in and greeted the Captain, but their eyes opened with sheer wonder when Pepper hailed them with, "Who are you? I'm Pepper." What a surprise for them all. The cats curled around Veronica's ankles, sitting as close to her as they could get.

Captain Schiff knew she was the right choice for him. She went to the kitchen to get some tea and cakes; while she was gone, he asked her father for her hand. Her dad hesitated as he thought the Captain didn't have such good financial prospects. Captain Schiff disabused him of that notion when he told of the vast treasure he discovered. He assured Veronica's parents he could take excellent care of her and adequately provide for all her needs. With that said, the father consented to the marriage.

Captain Schiff asked Veronica for her hand when she returned with the cakes and tea. He presented her with the necklace when she consented to be his bride. She was so shocked she dropped the pastries and spilled the teapot.

Licorice, Black Jack, and Pepper jumped down on the floor and started eating the cake's crumbs. "No matter," her parents said, "we are happy beyond words for you both."

Pepper, Licorice, and Black Jack liked Veronica and knew they would make an excellent family, and they hoped Veronica would spill more goodies in the future so they would get free eats.

Captain Schiff bought a lovely cottage in the suburbs close to his parent's property and decided to take a rest from sea travel, much to the chagrin of Licorice and Black Jack. They hoped soon he would tire of living on land and once again put out for sea, but until that time, they planned to stay with him, Veronica, and Pepper as a family.

With most of the money from the treasure, the Captain bought three boats and hired responsible captains with honest reputations. They selected crews with vast sailing experience and sterling papers, those who could do hard work while at sea. From then on, the Captain and his family would be assured of a steady income and would no longer have to worry about barely making ends meet.

The marriage took place in early May; many of the townspeople were there. While attending the reception, they observed Licorice, Black Jack, and Pepper reading Tarot cards. They were the sensation of the event. A month after the wedding, Captain Schiff's father passed away; not six months later, his mother became ill and died. It was a difficult time for the young couple. The cats and parrot tried cheering them up, but that was not possible. Only time could heal the grief they suffered from their family's loss.

The people of Liverpool pestered the young couple by the droves to receive readings from their pets. They did not respect the couple's grief or their need for privacy; they came by the dozens, day and night. They knocked on the door and trampled on the flowers in the front yard. They peered through the windows and parked themselves on the porch, refusing to go away until they received readings. They even visited on Sunday, which was considered a day of rest.

Finally, Benjamin and Veronica could take no more. After talking the problem through many a day and night, the Captain convinced Veronica to leave Liverpool and make her home temporarily on the Fair Winds. She thought it over and did not want to be separated from either him or their animals and decided to go with them on a new adventure.

They rented their cottage, and Captain Schiff gathered a new crew for the voyage, which was easy because of his honest and fair reputation. Before the official signing and before departing, he held a meeting with the seamen and explained that his wife, cats, and parrot were sailing with them. If they had any superstition about women, cats, or birds, he would suggest they not sign up on the ship, for that was how it would be. Every hand said "aye" and placed their mark on paper readily for the Fair Winds next excursion.

Licorice and Black Jack were thrilled. They would once again be sailing on the Fair Winds at sea, and not only that; they would be with their phenomenal family on another exciting voyage. Nothing could be better!

Pepper didn't care one way or the other she was part of the Schiff clan, and where they went, she would go. She also had a few secrets; she knew of several other treasure caches and might one day share the hush-hush information with Captain Schiff. It all depended on which the way blew!

Licorice, Black Jack, Pepper on the Black Pearl Voyage

Captain Schiff, the Master of the Fair Winds, a beautiful merchant sailing ship, was the owner of brother Bombay cats that were famous ratters. Their names were Licorice and Black Jack. They were born on the vessel, which acquired many exotic products sold in port cities worldwide. It sailed far away distances to trade goods. Once they received the imported products, the merchandise was exchanged for other products or sold to a requesting merchant, making a profit.

Captain Schiff was so proud of his cats that he had the figurehead carved with their likeness and ordered a fancy flag embroidered to depict them and herald their arrival at any port.

Licorice and Black Jack were twins who were jet black with luminous yellow eyes. They were identical except for their tails. Licorice had a fluffy wavy tail that undulated back and forth like a graceful fan. His brother, Black Jack, had a big crimp in his tail due to an accident he had chasing a rat. The problem made his tail move in a herky-jerky movement each time he wanted to fan it. Black Jack never got over the mishap; his tail had been his pride and joy. He swore to eradicate all rats with whom he ever came into contact. Thus, the Fair Winds was kept "rat-free" after intense hunting and several days at sea.

Many a ship's captains wanted to purchase the cats because of their adeptness at stalking and ridding any area of rats and the frolicsome entertainment they provided the crew. Captain Schiff said he was never going to sell them, for they were members of his family and were his pride and joy.

The cats had some harrowing adventures by being stolen after skipping ship. They had to be found and ransomed back. However, the Captain loved his cats and would have paid any amount of gold for their release. Not only were the felines famous in every port for being world-class ratters, but they also learned to tell fortunes by using Tarot cards on one of their lengthy, naughty excursions.

Captain Schiff also had acquired Pepper, the Parrot, from a marooned drowning pirate crew. Not only could the bird talk but, Licorice and Black Jack taught her to tell fortunes by using the cards. Between the three animals, they entertained the crew daily with stories, fortune telling, wild tales of piracy, naughty lyrics, and general shenanigans performed by the intelligent pets. They were ever into devilment, and that's what made them beloved by the crew, the Captain, and his wife, Veronica.

Several months after Benjamin and Veronica Schiff wed, the Captain's parents both died. Simultaneously, the cats and Parrot's reputation about their card telling ability made them so famous that the Schiff's had no privacy or peace. Everyone wanted a reading.

Finally, they decided they would have to leave Liverpool and try to make their home aboard the Fair Winds for a time to get away from the demanding people of the town. When a sailor lived on a ship at sea, it wasn't easy to make a permanent home on land among landlubbers. The anticipation of seeing another country just over the horizon could be hypnotic to one with sailor's blood. The noise, hustle, bustle of the busy towns and villages was usually too much for them for any length of time.

Sailing had its very own rhythm, and it was peaceful and tranquil aboard a sailing ship. Sure, the sails snapped in the wind, while the yardarms creaked and moaned, the waves hissed and slapped against the sides of the moving boat constantly.

The grunts, snorts, and barks of whales, keening, ha, ha, ha, seagulls, and high-pitched whistles of a school of dolphin were constant, but those sounds were soothing to a sailor's ear. At times, there was absolute quiet aboard a vessel as it rocked side to side, propelling its way from one port to another to seek ever-distant horizons and new adventures.

Not so the case on land. The clamor of crowds hawking their wares, the screeching, cursing vendors, the fights and brawls of the drunkards as ejected from inns was endless. The clop, clop, clop of horses and ever-constant creaking wagons as they traveled the uneven, slippery cobblestone walks proved a daily event. Stray dogs constantly barked. The daily announcement of lamplighters and knock-uppers was ever there. The cries of the long song sellers and fishmongers, rag and bone men trying to sell their wares were ceaseless.

The church bells that rang maddeningly all day and night to announce the hour or make public any emergency that arose in the town were the noises that assailed one ashore. It proved to be an impossibility to sleep or even think a rational, calm thought.

The beautiful blue sky, fluffy clouds, moon, and stars obliterated by the "too-closely built" hodge-podge dilapidated houses and the hanging, gray, ragged half-washed clothes that were ever flagging in the feted listless breeze. The stink of the dead carcasses hanging from the butcher's shops made everyone who passed by ill. The foul odors from the animal droppings along every footway, nothing was clean.

Smoke belched from chimneys and covered everything with a patina of soot. The contents of the privy pots tossed out of the windows landed on misfortunate passers-by. That moment could occur at any time. What a nightmare! Grit covered everything with ash and dirt, and it was dismal, dreary. Nothing was clean. What dreadful horrors for a simple sailing man!

The animals didn't care about these things. They were members of the Schiff family. Where Benjamin and Veronica went, they would go. They were constantly fed and cared for, and it mattered not where their meals came from; they were warm, dry, and beloved by all. After staying on land, Licorice and Black Jack longed to sail again, for they were, after all, cats born on the sea that enjoyed their life aboard the Fair Winds.

Pepper was born in Africa and once owned by a band of pirates. Her sea travel was extensive. She had sailed for years and knew a lot about the wicked ways of men and brigands. She also held secrets of hidden treasure; one spectacular find she shared with the Captain on their last voyage. It made him financially comfortable. She thought she might reveal the location of another cache later, but at the moment, she would bide her time to see what events unfolded.

Meanwhile, she felt it better to tell some and keep some. As long as the Captain thought she knew more, she was sure he would not sell her or give her away. If he did trade her, she might need the information to pass to a new owner. One never knew what could save your life.

Pepper wanted to stay with the family all her life, which was her insurance to do just that. The bird didn't understand that the Captain thought of her as family, and no matter what she did or did not do, he loved her and would never sell her or give her away.

Because Pepper divulged the location of a buried treasure that once belonged to the deceased members of a pirate crew she once sailed with, Captain Schiff purchased three other sailing vessels. He had become a man of means and was able to ask Veronica's father for her hand in marriage. The father accepted, knowing the Captain would adequately take care of his daughter. Veronica agreed too, but she didn't care if he had money; she loved him dearly.

Before departing Liverpool, Captain Schiff made arrangements and signed contracts to have a Ship's Agent oversee his other vessel's affairs. Knowing the Fair Winds would be gone for such a prolonged time, the Captain needed an honest broker to conduct his business ashore during his absence. He also decided to rig the Fair Winds with guns and cannonball since they would be traveling in areas where pirates often cruised, searching for unarmed merchant ships.

The firearms were costly, but he thought it would be better to have them than to need them and be without them. The journey would take many months, so the ship required adequate provisions. The Captain also thought since his wife, the cats, and the bird was sailing with him, he would need an extra safety layer to protect them from other unpleasant experiences.

Once he arranged everything, he and his lady packed their luggage, accompanied by the animals; everyone boarded the Fair Winds. It was the first voyage for Veronica, his wife; all the other crew, cats, and Parrot had "sea legs" and were used to sudden storms and the Fair Winds' steady sway and rock. Licorice and Black Jack would be up to their rowdy, playful behavior. The sailors were delighted.

Some hands had already voyaged on the ship and had witnessed the animals in action. Others were first-time crew members who heard of the cats and Parrot and were looking forward to the entertainment they would provide. One thing, for sure, they knew they wouldn't be bored with the two fun felines and the rambunctious bird aboard.

This time the Fair Winds was en route to the Fiji Islands in the South Pacific. A world-famous jeweler commissioned the Captain to purchase twenty pounds of black pearls, of which the islands of the South Pacific were famous. A perfumier also hired him in Paris to buy two hundred bottles of Monoi Oil (gardenia blossoms soaked in coconut oil.) and twenty-five pounds of Copra. All of these items highly prized by the upper-crust and nobility of

Europe, and dealing in them could yield a significant profit if they were successfully delivered in excellent condition to the buyers,

The rats of Liverpool heard of the Fair Winds and its imminent departure for the South Pacific, and many rushed to take advantage of the passage. First, they knew it had to be full of good "eats" since it would travel such a long distance. They also were tired of the wet, raw temperatures of Liverpool and wanted to move where soft breezes and swaying palm trees abounded.

They were intrigued by billboards and pictures of Fiji in travel offices they haunted. They didn't know they were sealing their fates by boarding the Fair Winds, the ship that Licorice, Black Jack and Pepper, the Parrot guarded and patrolled. What a dreadful mistake they made. They were to meet their end from the most intelligent Parrot and the most famous ratters in the world!

Licorice and Black Jack were unaware they were going to host a massive population of rats from Liverpool! Used to handling the usual amount of visiting vermin, it appeared this time they would practically have an army of them! They did not know they would be working overtime to keep the rats from taking over the entire ship and destroying all the food stored for the voyage in the hold. This trip wasn't going to be a casual, fun cruise, not indeed; it would be a "working overtime, drudgery" session for the cats if they were to keep the rodents from destroying everything. Ugh, they were not looking forward to that.

The Parrot would be working overtime too by serving as their eyes and screaming out to Licorice and Black Jack when she sighted a rat anywhere on the deck of the ship.

Not more than two days out of port, several of the sailors fell ill with a case of dysentery. There was food spoilage and eaten before anyone became aware of it. The remaining hands had to work twice as hard to keep the vessel sailing on its course and maintaining its favorable schedule. Captain Schiff, being a fair commander, didn't push the sailors beyond their capacity to work. He was mightily upset with the situation. He didn't, like some captains, blame the crew when things went awry. He knew there was absolutely nothing he could do to remedy the state of affairs, so he spoke to the seamen civilly hoping, time would cure it.

The circumstances were problematic at best. To make things worse, the "Cookie" was among those ill and could not perform the kitchen duties. Everyone was hungry and cross. No one else knew anything about cooking, so they prayed day and night that he would get well quick, fast, and in a hurry. Veronica, the Captain's wife, was violently seasick and could not help with the galley tasks or aid sailors who were ill.

Meanwhile, Licorice, Black Jack, and Pepper had no time for play. They raced hither and thither all over the boat, chasing and catching rats. The Parrot squawked continually, revealing a rat sighting. The vermin received no rest; they had second thoughts about being stowaways on the Fair Winds. At sea, it was too late to jump ship. They just hoped the boat would dock somewhere. Then they could depart before they were only a memory. Black Jack, most of all, was having the time of his life. He was able to fulfill his vendetta against the dastardly rodent population, which suited him just fine. A good rat was a dead rat was his motto.

Pepper tried cheering everyone up with pirate lyrics, but the men having to perform double duty made to eat unappetizingly, half-cooked food made the seamen cranky. They began to pick fights with each other, and it was all the Captain, and the first mate could do to keep them from injuring each other. Finally, it looked as though the ailing members of the crew were feeling better and were going to commence their assigned chores; what a relief everyone thought. They were all delighted to know the "Cookie" was going to return to his culinary duties before everyone got sicker or "starved" to death or were too weak to work!

No sooner than that good news occurred, the sky suddenly darkened. Winds began to howl, and the ship tossed as though it was a toothpick from gale winds of 70 to 100 miles per hour. Nothing was stable; everything aboard came loose and unfettered. The ship pitched from side to side. When the vessel leaned on one side, only the sky was visible; then, just the ocean was in view when reeling to the other. It was all the crew could do to keep hanging on and hope they would not lose their lives by being swept overboard or the ship sinking due to the enormous, towering waves. There was no possible way of controlling what was happening to the Fair Winds. The storm came up so rapidly that they did not have time to prepare for it by lowering the sails; winds ripped them to sheds. Only the masts were left naked in evidence to what had once been. Most of the seamen had experienced storms before, but none like this. All hands prayed for deliverance.

Licorice, Black Jack, and Pepper hunkered down in the hold with the remaining rats, declaring a truce until calmer times. No time to catch anything; they just had to hang on for dear life and hope this would be over before too long. The storm did not accommodate anyone and was in no hurry to depart, and it hung around several hours. It keened, wailed, screamed, and screeched so loudly most of the seasoned seamen were frightened this was beyond any experience of theirs.

Many of the crew thought they would lose their minds. Most of the ship's stores were swept into the greedy, grasping sea, to be lost forever. Fortunately, the lifeboats were secure and not lost during the raging turbulence.

At last, after many hours, the storm subsided. Everyone was weary and beyond their endurance. The Fair Winds was torn and broken. There was not one dry place aboard; even the Captain's quarters were soaking wet. The vessel wallowed from side to side, desperately trying to become even-keeled again. After the storm, the winds calmed, and the boat stalled. The crew had very little rest; all were working to keep the Fair Winds from sinking.

Once the ship shut down, the staff was unable to navigate in any direction. There was nowhere they could go as most of their canvas sails were in tatters. They could not notify anyone of their plight as they were mid-sea, and no boats were sighted anywhere on the vast horizon.

Bird owners, who do not want their feathered friends to fly away, clip their wings. Captain Schiff did this with Pepper regularly; however, he forgot to do so with all the hullaballoo of preparing for the Fair Winds' voyage. His having forgotten proved a blessed event.

Pepper, hearing the crew bemoaning their state of affairs, figured out she could probably fly off to see if there was any land nearby. She thought if an island was sighted, help might be obtainable for them. With that thought up, the Parrot rose and quickly flew out of sight. The crew tried to catch her, but she was too fast for them.

Every member of the team and Captain was devastated. Licorice and Black Jack jumped up on the side of the ship and searched as far as they could see; to no avail, she had disappeared entirely. Everyone thought she was lost forever. Not only were they in what looked like a hopeless situation, but Pepper had flown away, who knows where.

A whole night passed, the Fair Winds drifted in circles; in the morning, the sun bore down mercilessly, scorching everyone and everything. Water was becoming scarce as many of the casks were swept away. Nerves were fraying. It was a difficult time and dangerous to be aboard a becalmed ship! There didn't appear to be any help in sight.

Once a bird escaped, they were lost forever. Most birds like being free and hate being caged. Pepper, on the other hand, had had too much freedom with the dreadful pirate crew. She just wanted to stay close to her family, cage or no cage. Just when everyone lost hope, they sighted a dot in the sky; as it got closer, they realized it was Pepper! She landed on the boat and squawked "Land Ho." The crew couldn't believe their ears. They called the Captain, who was in his cabin studying maps attempting to determine their location. When he arrived on deck, he was astounded. His bird had returned. "What?" The Captain asked.

"Land," repeated Pepper as she rose again and madly flapped her wings up and down while facing the starboard side of the ship.

The Captain, first off, was delighted to see Pepper since he thought she was lost forever. His next idea was she probably did discover some land, and he needed to gather a crew and man a lifeboat in the direction she indicated. If it were true, they might get help from their dreadful situation.

He needed eight of his most reliable crew members who were proficient in firearms, for he didn't know what sort of people they would encounter upon landing. He had the sailors draw straws to see who would accompany him and who would stay aboard the Fair Winds. Once done, he provisioned each sailor with guns, sufficient ammunition, and sacks of dried fruit for their scouting trip and bid Veronica goodbye.

He left Licorice and Black Jack with her to not only keep her company but to protect her while he was gone. The cats were great for clawing, biting, and nipping the heels of anyone they thought needed it. They were loving pets but could prove to be ferocious when the situation called for it, and a family member became threatened. Captain Schiff and his hands boarded the lifeboat and rowed off with Pepper flying overhead.

They towed an empty boat with them if there was any edible food worth gleaning on the island with which to return. Since the destruction of so much of the food goods happened during the storm, Captain Schiff didn't want to miss the opportunity if they found anything worthwhile. The likelihood might be remote, but the Captain thought that was sound thinking, just if they were lucky.

After rowing all afternoon, they sighted a small island, one with a tall, elevated peak that appeared to be churning out billows of black smoke. What on earth? thought the Captain.

As they approached it, they discovered an active volcano was emitting the smoke. It seemed to be mountain size, and fortunately for them it was a considerable distance from the seashore. Finally, they landed on the beach and secured both crafts securely up in reeds, away from the tide. It would never do for their boats to sweep away while they were investigating the island.

The explorers began searching the area for people, taking care since they did not know if any wild animals were present or if the natives, if any, were friendly. They decided to stay together for fear of being ambushed. A man appeared out of a copse of trees, his clothes were in shreds, and he was hatless and barefooted. He approached the Captain and crew with delight. He told the sailors he was a master sailmaker, and his ship was smashed by rocks on the starboard side of the island several months ago.

He was the only survivor. He had the presence of mind to harvest several huge pots and a crate of bowls that were afloat from the wreckage. He also salvaged a few fishing nets and all the sails from his ship, and he used some of the cloth as cover when it stormed. Miraculously this was going to be just what the Fair Winds required. Not only did the man say he could make and repair sails, but he had several rolls of canvas that might do the needed job. Will wonders never cease, thought Captain Schiff.

After explaining their circumstances to the shipwrecked man, he said he was grateful but not surprised to see them because the area where they were sailing was known for massive storms, like the one that almost destroyed the Fair Winds. Many ships were wrecked and lost due to the dreadful maelstroms.

He told the Captain his name was Ramsey, and all of his crew members had perished. Unfortunately, his shipmates could not swim, and everyone drowned. The seamen noticed the island was full of a vast number of beautiful tall trees with round grapefruit-sized produce. Ramsay said it was called breadfruit. He also hauled several casks of water from the wreckage that was beached onshore and offered the sailors some of it.

Everyone was thirsty and appreciative of the gesture. Ramsey mentioned he had discovered a clear lake on the island's port side and was able to fill his casks whenever he needed to do so. He offered them something to eat and roasted several of the round green fruit. He cooked over an open fire and served eels, green turtle soup, and breadfruit to them. They felt close to starving and thanked him profusely.

Scrounging for fallen seeds and berries, Pepper nibbled them until full. The Captain shared his water with her. She flapped her wings and nodded her head in thanks to him. He told her he should be thanking her, for without her flying and searching for the land; they would probably have died aboard the Fair Winds.

Ramsey spoke of the volcano smoking and rumbling day and night and of his fear that it would erupt before being rescued. If that happened, he would have had no place to escape and would have died during an eruption by the hot molten lava. If the lava rolls down and reaches the seawater, it is so hot it can heat it to the boiling point.

Trying to escape by swimming away is fruitless; one could burn to death even if they are in the water. He thought before he arrived on the island, it had spewed fire showers because much of the sand was hot underfoot, and walking on it was impossible. There had been several small earthquakes during his stay, and they appeared stronger each time they occurred.

The Captain offered to sign him on the Fair Winds as a member of his crew, with the expectation that once they returned to the ship, he would immediately begin remaking and repairing their sails. Ramsey readily agreed he didn't want to remain on the island a moment longer than necessary. He helped the seamen gather bushels of breadfruit. He then showed the Captain several cages of palm leaves he wove during his stay; for the remainder of the day, they caught and placed sea turtles and eels in the baskets.

They loaded casks with fresh water from the lake Ramsey had discovered. Luckily, they had the second boat, and they chocked it to the brim with canvas, water, and all the foodstuffs they could gather. The return trip was uneventful.

Just as they were about to board the Fair Winds, they heard a roar and felt a powerful tremor. The lifeboats rocked furiously, almost tipping over. Upon looking back in the island's direction, they discovered the volcano had erupted and was spewing fire, boulders, rocks, and ash out of the funnel of its crest. The billowing black smoke, fumes, and flames were visible for miles. Ramsey could not stop thanking the crew for saving him from such a horrible fate as to be burned to cinders. They were also delighted they had departed in time. From the sounds it was making, it appeared that there would be no habitation or even an island, for that matter, in existence when the explosions ceased.

The sailors aboard the Fair Winds were delighted to see the returning crew. Licorice and Black Jack could not stop licking their chops in anticipation of some of the cooked eel. What a treat, they thought. Everyone welcomed the thought of freshwater, eels, turtle soup, and breadfruit. Cookie didn't know how to prepare the fruit, so Ramsey instructed him, and they had an excellent meal that evening.

The following day Ramsey went immediately to work. Tirelessly he labored it was an arduous task for him to make all the sails for the ship. Ramsey enlisted the cabin boy to help him sew some of the basic stitches. That way, the sailmaker was able to work faster than the canvas master would have had he just stitched it alone. Not having enough fabric to complete the job, he could, however, outfit her main masts, and the ship was able to move along.

It sailed at a slower pace than it would have if it had been at full mast, but no one complained. They were floating, they had food and water, and leaving a dangerous South Pacific area. As they departed, they saw the volcano was still furiously showering the air with fire and fumes. What a terrible place, they all thought.

Pepper did an excellent watch job by calling out sneaky, slippery rats when she spotted them. She cavorted again and sang more raucous songs to the crew's delight. Licorice and Black Jack resumed their ratting duties, and there was no lack of work for them to do. The little buggers were everywhere; there never seemed to be an end to them.

The cats squeezed in a bit of time to bedevil the Cookie for tidbits and tease the seamen by jumping off the masts on any unsuspecting head available. The older sailors knew to be wary of the felines and wore caps to keep from being scratched, but the new hands were not knowledgeable of their pranks. They drew gales of laughter from the old sailors when Licorice or Black Jack pounced on an uncapped dome and startled the unlucky one as they tried to duck for cover.

Veronica, by this time, became well and stayed outside of the cabin most of the time. Her presence tamed the seamen, who had to be on their best behavior. No disorderly rude conduct and certainly no cursing were allowed. It seemed strange to be aboard a sailing vessel at sea and watch what one said, but everyone adjusted to the new rules. Upon signing, the crew knew that the Captain's wife would be on board, and those aboard chose to control their raucous behavior. All hands agreed to it, so there were no surprises about that.

They sailed on toward Fiji and were grateful for full-blown breezes most of the way. Even though the Fair Winds had missing sails, she was able to cruise at a decent pace. The breadfruit lasted for several days, so they did not have to dig into their remaining dried fruit supplies and hardtack. The entire crew was happy about that fact because hardtack was not something they looked forward to eating.

Finally, they arrived at Tahiti, where black pearls were known to be available in vast quantities. No rats were left on the ship, being killed by Licorice, Black Jack, and Pepper. After docking, the Captain went ashore and found a mast supplier who sold canvas by the bulk. He asked Ramsey to accompany him, for he knew what would be a fair price for the material and how much sailcloth would be required to fit the masts.

The dealer knew that the Fair Winds members were desperate for the fabric, so he attempted to overcharge them. The Captain calmly told him if he did not quote a fairer price, he would spread the word about his dishonesty at every port the ship visited, and he would find his business to be non-existent in the future. The seller changed his mind and sold the cloth to them at a reasonable rate.

Captain Schiff rented a cart with a donkey and driver to haul the cloth back to the Fair Winds. Ramsey returned immediately with it and continued to repair and fit the sails. Meanwhile, the Captain asked where he could locate Mr. Rondo, the seller of black pearls. He was directed to the dealer and negotiated a reasonable price to buy twenty pounds of the beads. He carefully looked each of the gems over, as he did not want to return to the buyer with an order of defective goods.

By the time he left the black pearl dealer's and reached the ship, the vessel was in a total uproar. Squawking loudly, Pepper demanded everyone immediately fix things and get the situation in hand again. Veronica had a dreaded fear of rats and was screaming to high heaven, and the sound peeled throughout the streets of the port town. The Captain rushed to the ship to see what the problem was.

Never had his wife emitted such frightening sounds, never was there a time when she has made such ominous noises. Indeed, the ship must be on fire! Why was she having a hissy fit? She was a lady and always acted in a mild, subdued fashion. He couldn't imagine what had gone wrong. What on earth could be happening? Why weren't

Licorice, Black Jack, and Pepper looking after her as he requested? He wondered if the entire world had gone mad.

It appeared that upon the ship's arrival in Tahiti, the native population decided to rid themselves of all vermin that plagued them once and for all. The entire island overran with the rats. These killing operations made the rodents want to escape and save their lives. That day, unfortunately, the Fair Winds was the only ship docked in the harbor. Several other vessels had just departed, leaving Captain Schiff's boat vulnerable to boarding. The rats discovered the craft.

Subsequently, a horde of the vermin rushed madly aboard her to keep from being eradicated. The crew was being knocked down, tripped over, falling, slipping, tumbled, jostled, crushed, pushed, and shoved every-which-way, making an effort to get out of the way of the deranged horde of vermin and avoid stepping on the rats, cats, and a parrot.

The pets had gone wild and were attempting to catch each rodent as they dashed back and forth all over the deck. Several fat rats turned around and fled down the gangplank, back to land away from the dangerous hubbub. In a rush, the cats mindlessly followed them and landed on shore yet again without meaning to. Off they dashed madly chasing the pests, never stopping to think of the consequences of their rash actions. Their only thought was killing all rats! "We are the prize ratters of the world, and that is all there is to it."

The Chieftain of Tahiti, Teina, was being transported on gorgeous silk pillowed palanquin past the dock on the burdened shoulders of some of his struggling subjects. All stopped, mouths agape. They were astounded, watching two black cats in action and discovering how proficient they were at dispatching the legion of running rodents trying to escape to no avail.

The Grand Poohbah decided he wanted the felines captured for his exclusive use. His attendants readily agreed to try to catch them. He merely told his subjects, trying isn't good enough, do it, or off with your heads! Scared wasn't the word; they knew he was good at his threats. Many of his other subjects had lost their heads for lesser crimes. They gently sat the palanquin on the ground with the elephantine-sized Chieftain and immediately rushed to do his bidding. Of course, they were eager to comply with any of his demands with the threat of losing their heads.

They knew if they caught the felines, the boss would be happy, they would get to keep their domes, and Licorice and Black Jack would be a great solution to their massive rat problem. After quickly coming to that conclusion, they seized large fishing nets from a nearby merchant. The storekeeper raged as they did not pay; they just merely snatched a bunch of his netting and dashed off.

The thieves dragged it across the town center as Licorice and Black Jack raced round and round crazily, unaware of the trap. After chasing up and down the streets, the cats were suddenly snatched up and tangled in the mesh. Woe is us; here we are in trouble all over again, when will we ever learn, wailed Licorice and Black Jack.

The jeweled fingered obese Chieftain was delighted; he clapped his hands in sheer delight. His entire body jiggled whenever he moved. Oh, the joy of it, he chuckled; now we will be able to rid Tahiti of all its vermin. We once again will be able to sleep without them climbing all over us. They are in our food, our beds; they gnaw on and are in everything. They make a mess with their filthy droppings, multiplying countlessly and are spreading disease everywhere, to say nothing of frightening the children and all the natives of the land.

These wretches are out of control; however, with these lovely little cats doing their work, we can become rat-free for the first time in the island's history. Halleluiah!

After they clean out Tahiti, we can sail with them to the other Fiji Islands and offer them there. We can charge whatever we want to every isle Sub-Chieftain for the job, get rich, and rid the land of all the rats at the same time. What a grand idea! The group hurried back to the palace, secured Licorice and Black Jack in a giant cage. They then enlisted a group of workers to weave halters and collars of hemp to leash the cats. Licorice and Black Jack were pacing up and down, trying to figure a way out of this dilemma. Once again, they couldn't discover a solution to the mess in which they found themselves.

Meanwhile, Captain Schiff chased the rats out of his cabin and calmed his wife. He then went out to look for Licorice, Black Jack, and Pepper. He was going to give them a piece of his mind. The bird was sitting on the deck, with droopy feathers and head down. She was utterly crestfallen and uttered only, "Lordy, Lordy; they've gone."

The crew explained that the cats had taken off again, chasing several escaping rats down the gangplank; they admitted the cats were too fast to be caught by any of them. They apologized, but the Captain, knowing his Licorice and Black Jack, didn't blame anyone for their loss. They were undoubtedly speedy little devils. That's how they always catch their prey; speed was the answer to their success.

In the absence of Licorice and Black Jack, many of the rodents were left unchecked. They were running helter-skelter all over the ship, getting into everything. All the rodents acted as if they dared anyone to catch them. They seemed to be chanting, "bet you can't find us." It looked as though they were celebrating the absence of Licorice and Black Jack and trying to get away with as much as possible. Happy day, they thought; no more worries about being killed on land or this ship either. This situation is just our "cup of tea."

Captain Schiff stationed a cabin boy to stand watch in front of his cabin door. He gave the lad a broom to chase away any errant rodent that dared to enter his quarters. He had enough of Veronica's fear and wanted to alleviate her concerns as much as possible. Being her first voyage, it appeared that everything had gone wrong that could. It hadn't been the romantic trip he had promised her; it had been anything but that. What a harrowing experience they had had. Storms, torn sails, little food, no water, rats, lost cats, he prayed nothing else untoward would occur and hoped it would be smooth sailing for all of them from then on.

The vermin discovered the remaining foodstuff and tore most of the bags to shreds. They then proceeded to guzzle down and gorge themselves on everything edible. Captain Schiff would have to purchase an entirely new store of food for their return trip. He had also to buy many of the items that were swept overboard during the dreadful storm they experienced. Lord, he thought, where on earth are the cats? They'd better get here soon before we are ruined.

The Captain took several sailors with him to scour the town to look for Licorice and Black Jack. They searched everywhere to no avail. Upon seeing a woman on the street weaving baskets, they stopped to query her and ask if she had seen anything of them. Her name was Afaitu; she appeared delighted to divulge what had occurred when the cats disappeared. She was a widow who had only one little daughter, Mohea, who she loved deeply.

The child was so beautiful that everyone spoke of her loveliness everywhere. The Chieftain heard about her and had snatched her away at a very early age without her mother's consent. He planned to make her one of his brides when she came of age. The mother never saw the little girl again.

The Chieftain was known to do this anytime he saw a beautiful young child. All the natives tried hiding their attractive youngsters, fearing he would notice and would steal them. The parents cut their progeny's hair in an unattractive fashion, dressed them in rags, and made them wear scarfs and thick veils over their faces so that they would go unnoticed. The Chieftain had soldiers sweep the country-side regularly searching for beautiful young girls to capture for his harem.

All the natives hated him, but there was nothing they could do to stop him from taking their children. The thought of their babies living with and being married to the fat, gross, ugly, dirty old man was more than most people could bear.

Seeking her daughter, Afaitu was told not to come there or ever ask about her again. The palace guard said if she queried about the young person's whereabouts, she could be imprisoned, burned to death, fed to sharks, or beheaded. She could select whatever way she wanted to die; they would let her choose. She left, bereft, and prayed daily for something to happen to deliver her child back to her. So far, nothing changed, the girl was gone, and she lived in fear for herself and her daughter.

Once Captain Schiff knew what happened, he was livid. "First," he said, "those are my cats; they are my family," he screamed. "How dare anyone take them and make them prisoners for their greedy ends. Secondly, what is wrong with a person who rips a child from its mother and makes plans to wed her without her parent's consent? We'll just see about that," he said, and he and the crew accompanying him marched swiftly off to the palace situated in the center of the town. When they arrived at the palace gates, they found them shut. After knocking and calling out several times, a guard came to the gate, opened the small, hatched door encased in it, peeped through, and asked what the Captain wanted.

Captain Schiff said, "I demand my cats be returned to me this instant, Licorice, and Black Jack belong to me, and no one has the right to withhold them from me." The guard shouted, "go away" and slammed the little door.

Captain Schiff was enraged; he walloped the door several times with his fist. Finally, it opened, and there stood before him a group of palace guards. The Captain and his crew stepped forward, and the soldiers divided their ranks to permit them to enter. Once inside, the sailors and

Captain were surrounded and marched inside the building. Substantial ornate doors opened silently and revealed Chieftain Teina.

The chief perched on a mountain of silk embroidered cushions. The Grand Poohbah looked like a massively inflated balloon. In all of his travels, the Chieftain was the fattest creature the Captain had ever seen. He leered at the Captain while stuffing his fat face with delicate pastries. Cream and jelly filling was dripping off his chin and smeared on each of his jeweled fingers. It fell down the front of his robe. His hair spread with sugar, crumbs, and flakes of cake; he was a mess. He seemed not to notice. Between bites, he wanted to know why he was being disturbed at tea time and asked what the Captain wanted.

The Captain again requested he free his cats. The Chieftain belched loudly and said, "the cats are mine, I found them on my property, and finder's keeper is the law of the land. You have no rights here. I can quickly deport you or forbid you to land here ever again. I can also set your boat on fire, and then you would be stranded with no way to leave. That would make you destitute; you would have no way of making a living, so you would eventually become poverty-stricken, and according to my proclamation, that would make you a slave of mine. What's your choice? Forget about the cats, leave here immediately or suffer the consequences." His mouth was so full that he spat the food out on everything, everywhere; this was one disgusting character, thought the Captain.

Realizing that he was outnumbered and did not have the upper hand, the Captain said nothing but saluted the Chieftain in his best military manner, smartly turned on his heel, and departed with his crew. He knew this was not to be the end of the event but was keenly aware it was better to retreat than for him and his team to do something foolish they all might regret later and still not have his cats.

On the way back to the ship, Captain Schiff saw Mohea's mother again. She greeted him and asked if he was successful in retrieving his cats. She also wanted to know if he had seen any of the missing children; both questions the Captain answered no. He then spoke of what had occurred at the palace. She looked around cautiously and spoke in a lowered voice. The mother invited him into her hut and said she had something to discuss with him and didn't want anyone else to hear.

Once inside, Afaitu invited him to sit and take some tea. He was grateful for the respite and listened to what she proposed. She had several friends who had lost children to the Chieftain. Many of whom had relatives employed inside the palace.

The mother offered to talk with them to see if she could arrange to unlock the side palace gate doors so he and his crew could gain entry. Knowledge of the number of guards and stations was critical. The cats' whereabouts had to be known, as the palace was immense, and one could get lost in the winding corridors for hours.

Afaitu told him she could make no promises, as it was not her life on the line. Any caught servants would be tortured and killed. She wasn't sure if they would be willing to take that chance. She said it was their relative's stolen children, "and if it were me, and I had the opportunity, there would be no question of my seeking revenge. Of course, this was merely an idea of mine, and we will have to see what everyone else says."

The Captain was delighted beyond words. If she could round up the natives she spoke of, they could meet secretly in her hut, with the group later that evening to firm up plans, if possible. He thanked her and, with his crew, departed for the ship.

Nothing had improved in Captain Schiff's absence. The rats were continuing to run rampant. The sailors kept busy chasing them and trying not to get bitten when the rodents became cornered. Veronica stayed tightly shut up in their cabin, fearing to come out and encounter a rat. The cabin boy stood faithfully outside the Captain's cabin door beating off the rampant pests with his trusty broom. The entire situation was becoming unbearable. More and more rodents were invading the ship since they were aware Licorice and Black Jack were no longer there and were hunting onshore for the Chieftain.

The Captain thought the evening couldn't come soon enough. Hoping Afaitu could convince the palace servants to aid him; however, he wouldn't be angry if they refused. After all, the Chieftain was a cruel despot and had the reputation of having no pity or concern for anyone. The only thing he cared for was food, acquiring wives, and gold.

He didn't believe in the law of retribution. He only thought everything was his to take as he chose and would brook no intervention from another if they tried to stop him from his insatiable demands. The thought of giving something back never crossed his mind, take, take, and take this was his motto, always had been, and still would be, as long as he reigned.

Nightfall finally arrived. Captain Schiff selected twelve of his most trustworthy crew members. He outfitted each of them with knives, blunderbusses, flint, gunpowder, and shot. They crept off the ship under cover of darkness. They silently made their way through the darkened streets to Afaitu's hut. Upon arriving, the sailors waited outside while the Captain entered.

Inside were six natives, they were all eager to help free the cats, and they hoped they could release from bondage the children and some of the women who did not want to remain under the Chieftain's rule in the palace. All of the volunteers worked in the royal residence and were familiar with its layout. One person said he knew where the cats were; another provided a map, as he helped build an extension to the royal residence a while ago.

An arrangement had been made that afternoon to drug the soldiers in the palace, so several serving girls placed a mild opiate in the drinking water and wine. Providing it at dinner, all the palace guards fell drowsily asleep at their posts. The Chieftain tottered off to his quarters wondering why he was so exhausted, but after having had a humongous meal, he didn't question it too thoroughly; in no time he, also was fast asleep.

Everyone appeared eager to commence the raid. The Captain and his crew quietly made their plans. After an hour or so, they departed for the palace. When they arrived, one man knocked a pre-arranged signal on the large front door. The native who cared for the entry portal opened it and gave Captain Schiff and his crew entry. They followed the floor plan carefully.

The Captain followed the route indicated to free Licorice and Black Jack. Some sailors went to the Chieftain's bed chambers, while the others quietly stole off to the harem. Since the wives were aware of the plot, they did not drink the drugged liquid, so they were wide awake and alert when the sailors entered their quarters. The ladies were startled, but the raiders cautioned that they must be silent and not awaken the sleeping guards. The sailors said they were there to set them free if they wanted. No one wanted to stay; everyone wanted to leave. The chief's wives and all the young people followed the seamen out and were swiftly on their way to freedom.

Captain Schiff discovered the cage that held Licorice and Black Jack captive. He immediately released them and they, of course, jumped into his arms, mewing with sheer delight. The crew that stole into the Chieftain's rooms rudely woke him and tied him up without firing one shot. What a fantastic event that was, no one was hurt, and everyone was free.

Outside the palace, family members of all the harem residents waited. They greeted their long-lost relatives. Everyone cried for joy. The plan was to hold a meeting the following morning in the vast palace courtyard for every native in Tahiti who lost a loved one by the kidnapping scoundrel. Captain Schiff thought they might want to have a say as they had a vested interest in determining the fate of their captured Chieftain.

The guards were woken and herded into cells below the palace, where they were locked up temporarily—asking the women if they wanted to return to the castle or go to their family homes. All elected to leave. Everyone promised to come back in the morning for the trial of Chieftain Tiena. Captain Schiff thanked everyone for their help; they, in turn, thanked the Captain for releasing all the hostages. They were extraordinarily grateful to Afaitu for coordinating the plan and arranging for them all to meet. She was just happy to have her lovely little daughter back.

The Captain took Licorice and Black Jack back to the Fair Winds. They started routing the wild rats, and it was business as usual. Everyone on board was happy to see them, especially Pepper; she had sorely missed them. Now, hopefully, they would have order restored. She also hoped they would be sensible enough to stay on the Fair Winds and not "jump ship" ever again. Somehow that was probably expecting the impossible. In any case, they were back, and the Schiff family was whole once more.

The following morning Captain Schiff and several of his sailors returned to the palace. All the natives were there; they didn't want to be late and miss the momentous event. The natives selected a jury and brought the Chieftain out shackled hand and foot.

Everyone spoke of his misdeeds and how he had mistreated all the people under his control for many years. They voted and found him guilty of many crimes against the populous. He was sentenced to exile to a famous prison on Yaroua Island. They also sentenced six of his most cruel guards with him. His sentence was to last thirty years. Theirs would be five if they exhibited good behavior. He would have only their company, and they all could look forward to only meager meals once a day. They were all expected to work hard labor on work teams.

There was not going to be any joy in their future existence. All the Tahitian citizens were for the plan and bundled him, and his cadre of guards in a small boat and a few members of the Fair Winds paddled them off to begin to commence filling their sentences.

Once that was over, the natives decided to take a vote and elect a new Chieftain. After much deliberation, they agreed that Afaitu should be the reigning queen. The decision was unanimous. She, of course, was shocked but accepted the nomination. Afaitu made Captain Schiff an honorary member of Tahiti and told him he would be allowed to visit the island anytime and stay as long as he desired. Captain Schiff offered to let Licorice and Black Jack lose to run the island for several days. "That way," he said, "your island would be mostly free of rats."

She also hired two diving youngsters and told them to dive for pearls for ten days. She directed that whatever beads they found were to be given to the Captain as a reward for his ridding the island of Chieftain Tiena and freeing the native ladies and children. Everyone agreed with her decision and celebrated late into the night.

The following day, Captain Schiff shopped for the ordered foodstuffs, Monoi Oil bottles, and twenty-five pounds of Copra. The seamen cleaned and scrubbed the hold. They rid it of all the ruined produce and evidence of the army of rats that had visited there. Everything was in pristine condition when the Captain ordered them to weigh anchor and depart for Liverpool.

Veronica was ecstatic with the thought of returning home after such a long voyage. Ship life was not what she imagined, and the idea of being on dry land delighted her no end. Veronica hoped that her neighbors had forgotten all about Licorice, Black Jack, and Pepper's ability to read fortunes by this time. If not, maybe she could convince the Captain to sell their current abode and purchase another where they were not so famous. She had had enough notoriety; she just wanted a peaceful existence, if that were possible.

Afaitu and the natives all came down to the dock to bid the Fair Winds and the Schiff family goodbye. The sails filled with a great burst of air, and off they sailed out to sea, away from Tahiti harbor, homeward-bound which ever way the wind blows.

www.ingramcontent.com/pod-product-compliance
Lightning Source LLC
Chambersburg PA
CBHW071318130726
47996CB00002B/533